# PURRFECTLY DEADLY

## THE MYSTERIES OF MAX 2

## NIC SAINT

PUSS IN PRINT PUBLICATIONS

**PURRFECTLY DEADLY**

**The Mysteries of Max 2**

Copyright © 2017 by Nic Saint

All rights reserved. No part of this book may be reproduced in any form by any electronic or mechanical means including photocopying, recording, or information storage and retrieval without permission in writing from the author.

This is a work of fiction. Names, characters, places, brands, media, and incidents are either the product of the author's imagination or are used fictitiously. The author acknowledges the trademarked status and trademark owners of various products referenced in this work of fiction, which have been used without permission. The publication/use of these trademarks is not authorized, associated with, or sponsored by the trademark owners.

Edited by Chereese Graves

www.nicsaint.com

Give feedback on the book at: info@nicsaint.com

facebook.com/nicsaintauthor
@nicsaintauthor

First Edition

Printed in the U.S.A

# CHAPTER 1

*M*orning had arrived bright and early, and as usual I was having a hard time rousing my human. Odelia was still snoozing, even more reluctant than usual to throw off the blanket of sleep. She'd been stirring for the past hour, ever since her alarm clock had gone off and she'd unceremoniously silenced it with one well-aimed punch. In spite of all my nudging, meowing, and even scratching the closet door, she still showed no signs of getting out of bed.

She'd sat up half the night preparing for her interview today, but if she didn't get up now she'd miss it entirely. And it wasn't just any old interview either. For the first time in years, famous eighties pop singer John Paul George, aka JPG, had granted the Hampton Cove Gazette an exclusive.

John, whose star had shone so brightly back in the day, now lived as a recluse in his Hamptons mansion, only rarely venturing out. He was one of those pop deities and eighties icons whose name would go down in history along with Madonna, Michael Jackson, Prince and George Michael.

Originally he hailed from England, where they produce

pop stars in a factory just outside London, but had settled in the Hamptons in the nineties, where he could enjoy sun and surf and an endless parade of boy toys.

"Odelia," I tried again, nudging her armpit with my head. "Oh, Odelia. Rise and shine, my pretty. John Paul George and legend are awaiting."

But instead of opening her eyes, she merely mumbled something and turned the other cheek, her blond hair fanning across the pillow and her green eyes remaining firmly closed. I stared down at her sleeping form. I could always give her a gentle nibble, of course. Maybe that would do the trick. Somehow I doubted it, though. When Odelia is asleep, only a shot from a cannon can wake her, or perhaps a piper beneath her window, like the Queen of England. I should know. I've been Odelia's constant companion for going on eight years now. My name is Max, by the way, and I'm a cat.

Finally, I'd had enough. I wasn't going to miss this interview, as JPG was as much a hero of mine as he was of Odelia's. The man had taken in more stray cats than the Hampton Cove animal shelter, and all of them had been given such a good life they'd spread the word far and wide: JPG loved cats and they, in return, adored him. Heck, if I wasn't so fond of Odelia I might have presented myself on the JPG doorstep, looking slightly bedraggled.

I'd talked to more than a few of the cats he'd taken in, and they said he actually served them pâté on a daily basis. The food supposedly melted on the tongue, and was so delicious and plentiful it sounded like feline paradise.

The thought of pâté decided me. I wasn't going to miss the opportunity to sample the best gourmet food in all of Hampton Cove just because Odelia liked to sleep in. So I jumped on top of her, prepared to give her a good back rub, claws extended. If that didn't do the trick, nothing would.

Just then, Dooley wandered into the room.

Dooley is Odelia's mom's cat, a beigeish ragamuffin and not the smartest cat around. He's also my best friend.

"Hey, Max," he said now as he leisurely strode in. "What's up?"

"What's not up is the more apt question," I grumbled, gesturing at Odelia, who turned and clasped her pillow with a beatific expression on her face.

"Aw, she looks so sweet," said Dooley, looking on from the bedside carpet.

"We've got an important interview scheduled in an hour, and if she doesn't get a move on she's going to miss it."

"One hour? She can make that. Easy."

"Well, unless she gets up right now she won't," I insisted.

And then I got it. Maybe we could serenade her. Dooley and I had recently joined the cat choir. We got together once a week to rehearse, and even had our own conductor. We sang all the old classics, like *Cat's in the Cradle*, *Year of the Cat*, *What's New Pussycat* and things like that. The good stuff. Since we usually practiced at night, though, we were having a hard time finding a regular spot to get together, as the neighbors didn't seem to appreciate our nascent talent as much as we did.

"What was that song we did last night?" I asked Dooley.

He looked up at me. "Mh? What song?"

"For the cat choir. What was that last song we did? The one that made the mayor throw that old shoe at you?"

Dooley frowned at this, and rubbed the spot on his back where the shoe had connected. "That wasn't funny, Max. That really hurt, you know."

"Yeah, but what was the song?" I insisted.

"*Wake me up before you go go*," he said. "The old Wham! classic."

"Of course," I said with a grin. "Let's do it now. I'm sure

3

it'll be a nice way to wake Odelia up, and put her in the right mood for her interview."

I jumped down from the bed, and took up position next to Dooley. We both cleared our throats, just like our conductor Shanille, Father Reilly's tabby had taught us, and burst into song.

*"Wake me up before you go go,"* I howled.

*"Don't keep me hanging on like a yo-yo,"* wailed Dooley.

And even though we hadn't practiced the song a lot—the mayor's shoe had kinda ruined the moment—I thought we were doing a pretty good job. It probably wouldn't have carried George Michael's approval, as cats don't exactly sing like humans. When we sing, it sounds more like… a bunch of cats being strangled. Nevertheless, the effect was almost magical. We hadn't even gotten to the chorus yet, when Odelia buried her head in her pillow, then dragged the pillow over her head, and finally threw the pillow at us.

"Stop it already, you guys. You sound horrible!" she muttered.

"It's Wham!," I told her. "So it can't be horrible. And if you don't get up right this minute, you're going to be late for your important interview."

At this, she darted a quick look at her alarm clock, and uttered a startled yelp. The next moment she scrambled from the bed, practically tripped over Dooley and me, and raced for the bathroom.

"Shit shit shit shit shit!" she cried. "Why didn't you wake me?!"

"Well, I tried!" I called after her. "And failed."

"You think she doesn't like our singing?" asked Dooley, who's very sensitive about his singing skills. Coming after the shoe incident, Odelia's critique had clearly rattled him.

"I'm sure she loved it," I told him, padding over to the window.

4

Unlike humans, us cats don't need to spend time in the bathroom, or apply makeup, or put on clothes. We do spend half of our lives licking our butts, but apart from that, being a cat is a lot easier than being a human.

"I sensed criticism," Dooley said now, staring at the door through which Odelia had disappeared. "She said it sounded horrible, Max. Horrible!"

"She's not awake yet," I said. "She doesn't know what she's saying."

I hopped up onto the windowsill and watched the sun rising in the East. Outside, in the cherry tree that divided Odelia's garden from her parents', cute little birdies were chirping, singing their own songs, and fluttering gaily. I licked my lips. Coming upon the thoughts of pâté, the sight was enough to make my stomach rumble.

Dooley joined me, and we both stared at the birdies, twittering up a storm. There's nothing greater than waking up in the morning and seeing a flock of little birdies fluttering around a tree. It lifts my mood to such heights I can't wait to get out there and meet the world head-on. And the birdies. I saw Dooley felt the same way, for his jaw had dropped and he was drooling.

"So how's things over at your place?" I asked.

His happy gaze clouded over. "Rotten. That Brutus is spending more and more time at Marge's place than he does at his own."

Brutus was the black cat that belonged to Chase Kingsley, who was a new cop who'd recently moved to Hampton Cove. He was staying at Chief Alec's, Odelia's uncle, until he got a place of his own, but Brutus seemed to feel more at ease at the Pooles than at Uncle Alec's. And then there was the fact that he was dating Harriet, of course, Odelia's Gran's white Persian, who lived in the same house. One big, happy family. Except that it wasn't.

It had been a tough couple of weeks, Brutus being some kind of dictator, who liked to think he had to lay down the law to us plebeians. And since Dooley had always been sweet on Harriet himself, he was pretty much in hell right now.

"Brutus still being such a pain in the butt?" I asked.

Dooley nodded forlornly. "Last night he told me that from now on I should sleep on the floor. That all elevated surfaces were strictly reserved for him. Something about him having to have the best vantage point in case the house was being burglarized. I swear that cat is driving me up the wall."

"That's just plain silly," I said, shaking my head. Both Dooley and I had been wracking our brains trying to come up with a way to take Brutus down a peg or two. But as long as Harriet was his girlfriend, that was kinda hard, especially since Harriet is pretty much the most beautiful cat in Hampton Cove, and whatever she says goes with humans.

"You can always sleep on my couch, Dooley," I said magnanimously.

In spite of Brutus's efforts to take over my house as well, so far he hadn't succeeded. Fortunately Odelia still listened to me, and kicked him out when he became too much for me to handle. Oh, that's right. Didn't I tell you? Odelia is one of those rare humans who understands and speaks feline, on account of the fact that one of her forebears was a witch or something. Her mother and grandmother share the same gift, which comes in handy from time to time. Like when I have some scoop to share. You see, Odelia works for the Hampton Cove Gazette, and with the exclusive scoops we provide her she can practically fill the entire paper, earning her a reputation as the best reporter in town. She's also the only reporter in town, apart from Dan Goory, the Gazette's geriatric editor and Odelia's boss.

Finally, Odelia came shooting out of the bathroom, smelling deliciously of fresh soap, and looking fresh as a daisy. For the occasion she was wearing a T-shirt that read 'John Paul George for President,' beige slacks and her usual Chuck Taylors. She was also wearing a look of panic over how late it was.

"If you're coming, you better get a move on!" she yelled as she hurried down the stairs, then came pounding up again to snatch her smartphone from the nightstand and raced out again.

"Looks like she's going to have to skip breakfast," I told Dooley.

"And coffee," he said. "I wonder how she's going to survive without her daily dose of caffeine."

"I'm sure she'll manage," I said, reluctantly dragging my eyes away from the feathery feast outside my window, where the birds were still tweeting up a storm. Odelia had once made us swear never to kill a bird, and even though it killed us, we'd kept up our bargain so far. It was hard, though. Very hard. But in exchange for curbing our innate savagery she got us some of those delicious cat treats from time to time. What can I say? Life's a trade-off.

Dooley and I gracefully dropped down to the floor, and languidly made our way to the landing, then descended the stairs. While Odelia rummaged around, grabbing her notes she'd prepared for the interview, her recorder and a couple John Paul George CDs she wanted signed, and dumped it all into her purse, I gobbled up a few tasty morsels of kibble, took a few licks of water, and then waited patiently by the door until Odelia was ready.

I knew it would take her at least three runs to fetch all of her stuff. She was one of those humans who are extremely disorganized. So when she finally yelled, "Ready or not, I'm going!" Dooley and I had been waiting ten minutes. We were eager, actually. Hot to trot, in fact. It's not every day you meet your idol, and I knew Odelia was as excited as I was to meet JPG in the flesh. She because she'd grown up with his music, and I because I was finally going to find out if the rumors about that pâté were true. No matter who I had to bribe, I was going to sample me some of those delicious goodies.

Dooley and I hopped into Odelia's old pickup, and made ourselves comfortable on the backseat while she put the car in gear with a dreadful crunching sound that indicated she'd just destroyed what was left of the transmission. Miraculously, the car still lurched away from the curb, and five minutes later, we were cruising down the main drag of our small town.

Hampton Cove was just waking up, and Main Street was still pretty much deserted as we came hurtling through at breakneck speed. As a driver, Odelia is something of a legend in town. She's probably had more fender benders than all the other residents combined, and the only reason she hasn't been forced to declare bankruptcy to avoid paying traffic tickets is because her uncle is chief of police and tends to turn a blind eye to his niece's peccadillos. He has repeatedly told her to be more careful, but she insists the problem doesn't lie with her. She happens to be a great driver. It's other road users insisting on getting in her way that create all that trouble for her.

Meanwhile, we'd zoomed through Hampton Cove and were now racing along a stretch of road that took us along the coastline and the fancy mansions that the rich and famous had built for themselves. Dooley and I glanced out at them with relish. We had friends who lived here, and sometimes described the kind of lifestyle they'd grown accustomed to. It was enough to boggle the mind. Not that we're jealous cats, mind you. Odelia Poole is probably among the nicest and most decent and loving humans a cat can ever hope to adopt, but a monthly spa retreat just for cats? Cat birthday parties where all the other cat owners bring special treats? A walk-in closet just to fit all the costumes and fancy outfits? Like I said, it boggled the mind.

We finally arrived at the villa that was the home of John Paul George, eighties icon, and we were surprised to find that the entrance gate was wide open, a car haphazardly parked right next to it. As we rode past, we saw that inside the car a male figure was sleeping, his head slumped on the steering wheel, and recognized him as Jasper Pruce, JPG's long-suffering boy toy.

"Someone was naughty last night," Odelia said, lowering her sunglasses to get a good look at the guy. "JPG made him sleep outside, apparently."

"Don't humans usually have to sleep on the couch when they're bad?" asked Dooley, who looked confused. Human behavior often confuses him.

"Looks like the couch was occupied," I said, shaking my head.

We rode up to the house, and Odelia parked in the circular drive, right next to a fountain with a statue of JPG as a nude angel, spewing water out of its tush. We all hopped out and sauntered up to the front door. Odelia rang the bell, and we could hear it resonate inside the house. But even after she'd repeated the procedure, nobody showed up to answer, and she frowned.

She tried to peek through the glass brick wall next to the door, but it was impossible to get a good look because of its opaqueness.

She rang the bell again, biting her lower lip. "I hope he didn't forget about our appointment. It has taken me months to nail down this exclusive."

"Want us to have a look round the back?" I asked.

"Would you? I don't dare to go there myself. What if he's

9

sunbathing in the nude and accuses me of trespassing? I'll never hear the end of it."

Dooley and I moved off on a trot and rounded the house. We arrived at the back, where a large verandah offered a glimpse of the inside, but saw no evidence of anyone sunbathing, in the nude or otherwise.

"Oh, look," said Dooley. "He's got a pool."

And indeed he did. We walked over to the pool to take a closer look, and that's when we saw it: a lifeless figure was floating facedown in the center of the pool, completely in the nude, and judging from the large tattoo of two mating unicorns on his left buttock and a rainbow on the right, this was none other than John Paul George himself. I remembered seeing that tattoo when Odelia was researching the singer last night, and even though it looked slightly saggy now, having been tatted during the pop sensation's glory days, it was still recognizable.

John Paul George, eighties boy wonder, was either breathing underwater, or he was dead.

# CHAPTER 2

*A*fter we told Odelia what was going on, we pussyfooted back to the pool area, this time with Odelia right behind us. But even as we led the way, she told us, "This is a very bad idea, you guys. I shouldn't be back here."

It seemed like a weird thing to say for a top reporter, and I told her so.

"I don't know," she said. "Strictly speaking this is trespassing. And what's even worse, if what you're saying is true and John Paul George is dead and floating in his pool, I might get into a lot of trouble here."

It was the arrival in town of that new cop, I knew. The old Odelia wouldn't have thought twice about trespassing, and the fact that a famous celebrity was dead in their pool would only have made her run faster. But Kingsley's arrival had apparently robbed her of her journalistic instincts.

"Look, the guy invited you," I said. "So you're not trespassing."

"Well, that's true, I suppose."

"Besides, officially you don't know that he's dead. You

didn't hear it from us. You just wondered why he didn't answer the door, you got worried, and you thought you'd better check, in case something had happened to him."

"I like your thinking," she said, nodding. We'd walked around to the back of the house, and she gasped when she caught sight of the floating body. The last doubts as to whether the guy was snorkeling were removed: for one thing he wasn't equipped with a snorkel, and for another, no one can hold their breath for that long, and certainly not a fifty-year-old drug-addled pop star.

"Oh, God," said Odelia as she approached the pool. Then she proved that she was still the ace reporter I knew her to be: instead of a pool hook, she grabbed her smartphone and snapped a few shots of the deceased.

"Do you think he's dead?" asked Dooley.

"I think that's a pretty safe assumption," I said.

"Is it John Paul George?" was his next question.

I pointed at the tattoos on his behind. "See those tats?"

Dooley nodded. "Uh-huh."

"Only a pop star who's consumed massive amounts of dope and booze would ever even think of having those particular tattoos inked on his butt."

"Dope?" asked Dooley. "What is dope?"

"It's, um, like pâté for humans, only not as good for you."

"We have to call the police," said Odelia.

We all stared down at the floating body. The former teenage heartthrob was now twice the size he'd been in his eighties heyday. No wonder he was rarely seen these days, and never granted any interviews. One stipulation he'd given Odelia for her exclusive was no pictures, and I could see why. He probably wanted to preserve the image of his youthful self to his fanbase, not allowing them to see the extended version of himself he'd turned into.

Odelia pressed her phone to her ear, and when the call

connected, said, "Dolores? Can you tell my uncle there's been an accident at John Paul George's place? And tell him to send an ambulance. Yeah, he's dead."

While she gave the dispatcher some instructions, my eye wandered to the pile of glass vials on a table, the dozen or so empty champagne bottles on the pool chairs and the ashtrays full of reefers. That must have been some party.

"Oh, and can you also tell him JPG's boyfriend is dozing in a car in front of the estate. Maybe he's got something to do with this tragedy. Thanks, hon."

She disconnected and crouched down at the edge of the pool. It was obvious that the demise of one of pop music's greats had strongly affected her, to the extent she'd stopped snapping pictures, probably out of respect.

Just at that moment, a cat came walking out of the house. She was a beautiful Siamese, and said, "What's all this noise? And who are you people?" Then she caught sight of the man floating in the pool and faltered. "Is that…"

"Afraid it is," I told her, and watched her approach the pool wearily.

"Is he… dead?"

"Afraid so," I repeated, studying her closely.

She jerked back when the truth hit her. "Oh, no. Johnny's dead?"

"Looks like it," I said. "How long had you known him?"

The segue wasn't very smooth, I admit, but that's what you get from living with a reporter: you start acting like one yourself.

She shook her head distractedly. "Long enough to know that this isn't right." She plunked down on her haunches, and stared at her dead human.

"Is it true that he fed you guys pâté every day?" asked Dooley.

She looked up sharply. "What kind of a question is that? Who are you?"

"The name is Dooley," he said, scooting forward, probably to rub his butt against hers. But the look she gave him quickly dissuaded him.

"You're trespassing, Dooley," she said simply. "Please leave."

I shot Dooley a censorious glance and he lifted his shoulders. "What?"

"You can't ask the cat of a recently deceased human about pâté," I hissed.

"Why not? Isn't that what we came here for?"

"Well, you just can't," I whispered. Even though I was pretty curious about that pâté, too, of course. But there's a time for pâté and now wasn't it.

Just then, two more cats came sauntering out of the house, and then two more, and before we could say hi to the first bunch, we'd been joined by a dozen cats, and they all sat staring at the dead man. Then, as one cat, they all started mewling plaintively, letting their torment be heard across the pool.

Dooley gave me a curious look, but instead of explaining to him that this was what cats did when their owner suddenly passed away, and especially an owner as generous with the pâté as John Paul George apparently was, I decided to join in the ritual. After a moment's hesitation, so did Dooley, and before long, we were both howling along, our cat choir practice finally coming to good use. Even though JPG hadn't been our human, we could certainly understand the distress that comes with having to say goodbye to a beloved human, and as we mewled up a storm, Odelia simply sat there.

Soon, our howls mingled with the sounds of a police siren, and before long we were joined by Chief Alec, Chase

Kingsley, and other members of the Hampton Cove Police Department. They all walked up to Odelia and for a moment simply stood staring at us cats, as we continued our cater-wauling. Then, just as abruptly as we'd started, we broke off, and one by one the cats all drifted back inside. They'd said their goodbyes and the show was over.

Dooley and I decided to follow the others inside and glean what information we could from them. That, and we desperately wanted to take a look at the house, of course, and how the other cats lived.

The house itself was a genuine mansion, with nice hardwood floors and huge portraits of the singer adorning every room. The man had apparently possessed a healthy dose of self-love, for he was staring down at us from every wall in every room we passed through. I quickly trotted after the group of cats as they made their way to what looked like a family room. At least it was where a collection of cream-colored sofas were gathered around an outsized coffee table that held a collection of outsized coffee-table books, all sporting pictures of nude males on the covers and all visibly well-thumbed.

The cats hopped up onto the couches and the coffee table and made themselves comfortable. In one corner of the room stood a white grand piano, and here, too, several cats stretched out and chilled.

I decided to follow the Siamese, who seemed the only one willing to talk, and saw she'd sauntered into what looked like a recording studio off the family room. A lot of studio equipment indicated this was some kind of home studio, with an actual sound studio, recording booth and plenty of instruments placed against the far wall. I also saw enough gold and platinum albums to fill a hall of fame. This was JPG's personal hall of fame, that was obvious. The Siamese sat next to an acoustic guitar that was placed on the floor, next to a couple of bean bags, a stack of music paper nearby.

"Was this where he composed his music?" I asked.

She nodded, and appeared on the verge of tears.

"He was a great artist," I told her. "An icon of his generation."

She looked up sharply. "What do you mean, his generation? He was the musical icon of this century, and the last. The greatest living artist, bar none."

"Well, there are others," Dooley argued. "I mean, what about The Beatles? The Stones? Dylan?" He shut up when she gave him a dirty look.

"None of them were as influential and as talented as Johnny," she said, and it was clear we were dealing with an actual groupie here. A super fan.

"So what happened last night?" I asked, deciding it was perhaps better to grab the bull by the horns, or the Siamese by the ears, as was the case.

She shook her head. "He was partying hard, as usual. He'd just had another fight with Jasper, and he was overcompensating."

"Jasper?" mouthed Dooley.

"The boyfriend," I mouthed back. "We saw that. He's parked out front."

"That often happen?" asked Dooley.

She nodded. "They'd been fighting a lot lately. Jasper didn't like that Johnny consumed so much... candy. He said that wasn't what he'd signed up for. But Johnny said it gave him the boost he needed to create his music."

"Candy?" asked Dooley.

"Dope," I told him. "So Johnny still recorded?"

"Oh, yes, he did," said the Siamese with a smile. "Johnny must have recorded hundreds of songs since I came to live with him. All masterpieces."

"I'll bet," Dooley muttered, earning himself another scowl.

"When was this?" I asked.

She flickered her eyelashes at me. "Is that a roundabout way of asking me how old I am?"

"Um…"

"Johnny took in any stray that wandered into his home," she continued with a wistful smile. "But he got me from a proper breeder five years ago and I have the pedigree to show for it. Not that it matters." She sighed. "Johnny was the most generous human a cat could ever hope to come across. He loved all of his children, as he called us, and cared for us deeply." Once again, it looked as if she was on the verge of tears, and Dooley and I stared at her sheepishly.

I would have gone over and said, 'There, there,' but somehow I doubted whether this would go over well with this feisty and proud Siamese.

"Do you think there might have been foul play involved?" I asked instead.

She stared at me with her beautiful blue eyes. "I doubt it. Who would want to harm such a sweet and charming man? Everybody loved Johnny, and not just us cats. He had lots of friends, and partied every single night."

"What about his boyfriend?" I asked. "You said yourself he was jealous."

"Impossible. They might have had their differences, but Johnny and Jasper loved each other, in their own way. They had an understanding."

"Which was?" asked Dooley.

She eyed him angrily. For some reason she didn't seem to like Dooley. "I don't expect you to understand, but they gave each other freedom and respect. Jasper knew Johnny was an artist and needed his space, so he happily gave him what he needed. He knew Johnny would never hurt him intention-

17

ally, but that he had certain... needs, and so he turned a blind eye."

"Right," I muttered, remembering the pile of glass vials and the reefers and the bottles of champagne. I now wondered what had been in those vials.

"How many people were here for the party?" I asked.

She shrugged. "Maybe a dozen. Only one stayed the night, though."

"And it wasn't Jasper," said Dooley.

"Like I said," she snapped. "They had an understanding."

"Though last night they also had a fight," I reminded her.

"Yes, Jasper told Johnny he was fearing for his health. He was using too much and too frequently."

"Using what?" I asked.

"Some... substance. It came in clear glass vials. It made Johnny happy."

And now it had made him dead, I thought. "So who was the lucky young man who got to stay behind last night?"

"No idea. I was roaming the beach, and so were most of the others."

"So who—"

"George told me. George never goes anywhere."

"And who is this George?"

"He's Johnny's first cat. He brought him over from England years ago."

"George must be pretty old by now."

She laughed. "Don't tell him that to his face. George is very vain."

"Where can we find him?"

"You won't get anything useful out of him," she said as she started strumming the guitar with her nails. "George is extremely loyal."

"We'll see about that," I muttered. "Thanks, Miss..."

"Johnny always called me Princess," she said, and sighed. "I'll miss him."

I could very well imagine. If my human died one day, I'd miss her, too. Us cats might have the reputation we're selfish and we don't care about humans, but that's a filthy lie. We do care about our humans. We just don't care to show it as much as dogs do, with their exaggerated slobbering and posturing.

Dooley and I left the distraught Princess and made our way back to the family room, where the other cats were still looking glum. I wondered what was going to happen to them. I imagined JPG must have made provisions in his will for his beloved felines, and they would all be taken good care of.

"This makes me sad," said Dooley, gesturing at the sad-looking cats.

"Yeah, it's not a barrel of laughs," I agreed.

We both stared up at a life-sized portrait of the pop singer. It depicted him in his prime, with naked torso, looking like a young god. At his feet a large red cat sat perched, staring haughtily at the viewer.

I pointed at the cat. "I'll bet that's George."

"You want to have a chat with George? Or check out that pâté first?"

It was a tough choice. We'd come here for the pâté, obviously, but we also had an obligation to Odelia to find out as much as we could from the feline population about what had happened here last night. Finally, I said, "That pâté isn't going away, so we better talk to George first."

"Didn't you hear Princess? George has been here for years. He's the one who's not going away. That pâté might be gone by the time we find it." He shook his head. "A distressed cat eats, Max. It's called stress-eating."

He was right, of course. Still... "Look, this talk with

George won't take long, and I'll bet there's plenty of pâté. JPG didn't stint on anything."

"Why don't we split up? I'll look for the pâté and you look for George."

"Yeah, right," I scoffed. "So you can eat all the pâté? I don't think so."

"I wouldn't do that, Max. I'm not a glutton. I'd simply sample the stuff. Just to see if it's as good as advertised. And if it is, I'll leave some for you."

"That's very generous. You know what? I'll look for that pâté. You find George."

"You're a much better interrogator, Max. Cats open up to you."

"Why don't we find that pâté together," I finally suggested, "before it's all gone."

"Now you're talking. Hey, look," he said, gesturing at a lone ginger cat that shuffled out of the family room. It was the fattest cat I'd ever seen.

"That must be George," I said.

"Let's ask him where the pâté is," Dooley said happily.

"Good call," I grunted, a low rumble in my tummy deciding me.

Hey, we're cats. We're willing to do whatever it takes to help out our humans. As long as you keep us properly fed and hydrated.

# CHAPTER 3

*O*delia got up to meet her uncle and Chase. She'd been seated on one of the pool chairs, thinking deep thoughts about the fleetingness of life.

She gestured at the man floating in the pool. "This is how I found him."

"And what were you doing here, exactly?" asked Chase, none too friendly as usual. Ever since the burly cop had moved to Hampton Cove, he and Odelia had locked horns over his idea that the citizenry had no place in police investigations, whereas she felt she was simply doing her duty to the Hampton Cove population by reporting on any crime that was committed here.

"I had an interview with him, and when he didn't answer the door…"

"You decided to break in," Chase supplied.

"I was worried when he didn't answer the door," she said with some heat. Why did this guy insist on rubbing her the wrong way? "So, yes, I decided to walk round the back and see what was going on. What's wrong with that?"

"I don't believe you have to ask," he grumbled, shaking his head.

Uncle Alec knelt next to the pool. "That's Johnny, all right," he said.

"How do you know?" asked Chase, joining him.

The Chief pointed. "See those tattoos? Johnny was famous for those. They were on one of his best-selling albums. Unicorns and Rainbows."

"I remember," said Chase, nodding, and started singing softly. *"Unicorns and rainbows. That's the way the wind blows. Loved you in those funky cornrows..."*

Now it was Odelia's turn to give him a curious look.

"What? I loved that song," said Chase.

"I had you pegged as a country and western kind of guy. Not a JPG fan."

"Hey, I was young once."

"Hard to imagine," she muttered. She saw that her uncle was checking the glass vials on the poolside table. "What do you think those are?"

"If I had to venture a guess I'd say GHB," he said.

"Liquid G? The date rape drug?"

He nodded. "It's supposed to supply a great high. Used by ravers."

She imagined her uncle saw these drugs all the time during the summer, when teenagers descended upon the Hamptons in droves to party all night.

Chase walked over and eyed the vials closely. He put on plastic evidence gloves and carefully picked one up and sniffed it. "You could be right, Chief."

Uncle Alec nodded. "It's no secret that JPG was a heavy user of the stuff. It's been rumored for years he got his stash of GHB right here in town, but I've never been able to pinpoint who exactly his dealer was."

"If it is Liquid G," said Chase, "it might be what killed him."

More people arrived now, and Odelia recognized one of them as the medical examiner, a scruffy-looking paunchy man with electric gray hair. Under his instructions they carefully dragged the body of the late singer to the side, then hoisted him up out of the water and placed him on a plastic tarp. The sight was disconcerting to say the least, and Odelia uttered an involuntary gasp. She hadn't seen any pictures of the singer in years, and since he was completely naked, she now got to see all of him and it wasn't flattering. The man was bloated, and it wasn't because he'd been in the water all night either, she guessed. JPG had obviously let himself go, and looked nothing like his trim and sexy self. Of course that had been thirty years ago.

The medical examiner quickly and expertly checked the body, while Chase and Uncle Alec went over the crime scene, along with the other officers. Odelia, meanwhile, stood back. She might be there in a non-official capacity because her uncle allowed it, but that didn't mean she could actively participate in the investigation.

"Did you check the boyfriend at the gate?" she asked when Uncle Alec wandered over.

"Yes, we did. Apparently they had some kind of a fight last night, and he drove off, only to return and spend the night in his car. From what I can tell, it wasn't the first time. There have been complaints from neighbors about screaming fights the last couple of months. They were not a happy couple."

"Poor guy. He had to sit back and watch his boyfriend invite over these…" She gestured at the bottles of champagne and the vials. "Friends."

"Male escorts is the word," said Uncle Alec. "You don't

have to pay friends to have sex and party all night. You have to pay these guys, though."

"Kinda sad for a man like JPG to lead a life like this, don't you think?"

"Yes, well, if this was the life he chose, that was entirely his business," said the Chief, who believed in the age-old adage of live and let live, as long you didn't hurt others. It was a credo that helped him cope with the celebrities that lived in these beachfront properties, and sometimes liked to do stuff that no clean-living, well-meaning Hampton Covian would.

"What do you think happened?" she asked now.

He scratched his scalp. "I think Johnny had himself a great party here last night, lots of booze and dope, he overdosed and drowned."

"So you think it was an accident?"

He raised his eyebrows, and wandered over to the coroner. "Abe?"

"Well, he didn't drown, that's for certain," said the coroner.

Both Odelia and her uncle looked at him in surprise.

"No water in the lungs as far as I can tell," the coroner explained. "Though I'll have to get him on my slab to know for sure."

"Overdose?" the chief asked.

The coroner looked up at them from his position next to the body. "If it was an overdose it wasn't from GHB, if that's what you're thinking. This man died of a seizure of some kind. But like I said, I'll know more later on."

Both Uncle Alec and Odelia's eyes flashed to the pile of vials on the table.

The coroner nodded. "I'll have them examined. See what they contain."

Chase, who'd been checking around the pool area,

returned with two items dangling from his gloved fingers. One was a bright red Mankini, the other looked like a used condom. He gave the chief a grim-faced look. "Plenty more where this came from," he grunted. "At least five more."

"Some party," muttered the Chief. "Why don't you interview the boyfriend?" he suggested to Chase. "I'll have a look around the house." He turned to Odelia. "And you... why don't you do what you do best?"

She nodded her understanding. Uncle Alec was one of the few people in the world who knew about her ability to talk to cats, and with so many cats on the premises, there was a good chance one of them had seen something.

"And what is that, exactly?" asked Chase. "Snooping around?"

She gave him a thin-lipped smile. "That's right. I'm an ace snooper."

He shook his head, and muttered, "Unbelievable."

It was safe to say he wasn't a big fan of Uncle Alec's policy of including his niece in his investigations. But since he wasn't in charge, there was nothing he could do but grumble.

She passed into the house, in search of the cats, and found about a dozen of them looking glum and occupying couches and every other available surface in the family room. She took a seat to talk to them, but they merely stared at her with their sad eyes, and refused to acknowledge her presence.

Finally, she wandered on, hoping that Max and Dooley had had better luck. The house was just what you'd expect from a famous singer. At first glance, she saw a vintage guitar in a glass display case, and knew it was the guitar that had been on the cover of his first hit record. Huge portraits of the man were everywhere, looking as he did in his prime. This wasn't the house of a mere mortal, but a genuine star.

She arrived in the hallway, with its sweeping staircase, and wondered where Max and Dooley could be. The house was so big it was easy to get lost. She decided to venture upstairs and see if her cats were there. Ascending the stairs, she was careful not to touch anything, knowing the crime scene people would want to check the entire place for fingerprints.

Arriving on the landing, she saw several doors leading off the central hallway, and wondered how many rooms there could possibly be in this place. Every door sported an enlarged laminated reproduction of one of his album covers. For a moment, she stood poised, wondering where to start. Then, suddenly, she thought she heard a noise. It seemed to be coming from one of the rooms behind her so she turned and walked over. The door was ajar so she gently pushed it open with her elbow, and peered inside.

The first thing she saw was a huge multi-colored cockatoo, staring back at her from its perch in front of the window. So that explained the sound. And as she entered the room, she saw this was probably the master bedroom, as it was easily as large as a single floor of her own house. At the center of the room stood a large heart-shaped bed, with mirrored ceiling, and on this bed, she saw, rested the naked form of a very well-endowed young man.

He was fast asleep, in spite of the mutterings of the cockatoo, but then the large parrot reared up, spread its wings and took flight, screaming, "Come here, pretty boy! Come to Papa! Come to Papa right now, pretty boy!"

The young man suddenly jerked up, caught sight of Odelia, and started screaming, scrambling back against the wall, where a giant portrait of John Paul George had been placed, completely in the nude and looking buff.

"It's all right!" Odelia yelled, holding up her hands. "I'm a friend!"

But this didn't seem to console the young man, who looked like a male model, and was absolutely out of it. Probably still high from last night, she guessed, for his pupils were extremely dilated, and he seemed berserk.

He was probably one of last night's guests, and perhaps the last person to see the singer alive. His screams, meanwhile, carried through the open window and down to the pool area, and already she could hear footsteps pounding up the stairs. Moments later, Chase burst into the room, his eyes flying to the naked man on the bed. Then he caught sight of Odelia and shook his head. "I leave you alone for five minutes…"

The guy, taking a good look at Chase, now stopped screaming. "Hey!" he shouted, suddenly looking disgruntled. "What the hell are you doing here?"

"I…" Chase began, but didn't get the chance to continue.

"Were you with Johnny just now? Don't you know the rules, man?"

"What rules?" Chase asked with a frown. "What are you talking about?"

"The rules, man! The one selected by Johnny stays." He then slapped his sculpted chest. "I was selected, buddy. I get to stay. Not you. Me! I'm the one who gets paid the big bucks. So why don't you get the hell out of here?!"

"Wowowow," said Chase, finally grasping the man's meaning.

"He thinks you're an escort, Chase," said Odelia helpfully.

"Hey!" cried Chase. "I'm not… No way can you even think that I'm…"

"You're a pretty boy," said the escort. "But I'm prettier. Now beat it."

"Yes, pretty boy Chase," Odelia said. "You weren't chosen, so beat it."

"You, too, lady," said the escort. "Johnny's not into bony bitches, or any bitches, for that matter, so get the hell out of here or I'll tell the agency."

Now it was Odelia's turn to glare at the guy. "I'm not bony!"

"You're practically a stick figure," said the escort. He was right about one thing, though, and so was the cockatoo. He really was a very pretty boy.

"Look, I'm not an escort, all right?" said Chase. "I'm a cop."

"That's great. Who cares? Cops, firemen, construction workers. Johnny's tastes run the gamut. But this time he chose a college professor. Me!"

"You're a college professor?" asked Odelia.

The guy planted his hands on his narrow hips. "Don't I look like a college professor to you?"

"Not like any college professors I've ever seen," she said, remembering her own college days. The professors had all been woolly-headed hobbits. Maybe if they'd looked more like this guy she'd have paid attention.

"I don't care! I was chosen! Johnny chose me! Me! Me! Me!"

At this point, Chase must have had enough, for he suddenly pulled his gun, and pointed it at the self-declared college professor. "Hands up!"

"Oh, now you're talking," said the guy, still pretty hyped-up. "Are you gonna shoot me, cop? Are you going to take a shot at me?! Catch me if you can!"

And with these words, he hopped from the bed and before either Odelia or Chase could stop him, jumped out the window!

They both hurried over and stared down. The naked college professor lay sprawled on what had been JPG's terrace table, which had collapsed when he'd taken a running leap at it. Two uniformed officers leaned over him.

"Is he dead?" yelled Chase.

One of them looked up. "Nope."

"Too bad," grunted Chase, holstering his weapon.

And as both he and Odelia headed down, she said, "You could be an escort, you know, pretty boy."

He gave her a grin, which was the first time today. "Good to know I've got a backup career plan in case my days as a cop are over." Then he gave her a quick once-over. "And for your information, you're not bony at all."

"Thanks," she said, and felt a blush creep up her cheeks.

Just then, the cockatoo decided to join them. Shouting, "Come here, pretty boy!" he swung down and landed on Chase's shoulder. "Come to Papa!"

"Christ," growled Chase. "I hate this case already."

$\mathcal{W}$hile Odelia and Chase were otherwise engaged, Dooley and I hadn't given up on our mission to talk to George, JPG's First Cat, as the others apparently called him. We followed the ancient feline into an enormous kitchen, all gleaming surfaces and expansive kitchen block, and watched him waddle up to a nice row of bowls, all lined up against the window like soldiers on parade. There was a bowl for each cat in Johnny's menagerie, and they were jumbo-sized and filled to the brim. Whatever his faults, the man certainly knew how to take care of his felines. Eagerly, we approached the bowls. It wasn't kibble, like we got at home. It was something much better. Something squishy and tender. Something that smelled a lot like...

"Pâté!" Dooley cried enthusiastically. "I love John Paul George!"

I felt a strong urge to dig in and take what wasn't necessarily mine, but Odelia had raised me better than that. I would have liked to say the same thing about Dooley, but unfortunately I was wrong. The moment I turned my back, I heard distinct gobbling sounds, and when I looked back at my partner, I saw he was eagerly digging into a bowl that wasn't his. According to the name printed on the bowl in gold lettering, it belonged to Princess.

"Dooley!" I hissed.

"Wha?" he mumbled between two bites.

"You can't do that!"

"Oh, God, this is so good," he muttered, and simply kept on eating.

Shaking my head at so much foolishness, I trotted over to the far end of the long line of bowls, and joined George, who'd plunked down in front of his own bowl, and was feasting on his own portion with leisurely licks of his pink tongue. As the resident Methuselah, George was easily twice my size, and I'm not a small cat myself. His own bowl, aptly labeled 'George,' was also bigger than the others, and the one closest to the fridge. It was obvious that George was the *primus inter pares* in this small feline community.

I cleared my throat to announce my arrival. George looked up lazily, gave me a quick scrutiny, then dug his face into his bowl again and gobbled on.

"Hi, there," I said, as chipper as I could muster. It's hard to be cheerful when everyone is eating pâté and you're the only one left out, due to some personal moral code that I was now seriously starting to question.

This time he looked up long enough to utter a few words. He sounded like The Godfather, speaking as if he had cotton balls in his mouth. "And who are you then, brother?"

"The name is Max. I'm with Odelia Poole? She's the one who found…"

He shook his head, his chins quivering. "Sad state of affairs. Very sad."

"So you heard?"

"I did more than that. I actually saw how he died."

Bingo! "I'm so sorry for your loss," I said.

31

"Thanks." He heaved a rattling sigh and plunked down on his haunches. "It's a sad day for all of us here at Xanadu."

"Xanadu?"

"That's how Johnny called this place. He was a big Olivia Newton-John fan. And Gene Kelly, of course."

The reference completely went over my head, but then I wasn't as old as George, of course. "So what happened? How did he die?" I asked.

"Too much happy juice," he said, producing a tiny burp.

"Happy juice?"

"Oh, did he love the stuff. Took it all the time. I think it's safe to say he couldn't live without it, much to Jasper's chagrin. He hated the stuff."

"So too much happy juice, huh?"

"Yeah. It's like catnip to us cats, but for humans, and, unlike catnip, it's odorless. I should know. I once took a sniff of the stuff. No smell at all."

My mind flashed back to the vials. Of course. Happy juice. It must be the stuff that was in those vials. Some kind of drug, apparently.

"What a meal," sighed Dooley, sauntering over, still licking his lips.

I took one look at Princess's bowl and saw that Dooley had eaten the lot. Uh-oh. If Princess discovered her bowl empty, there would be hell to pay.

"So you think Johnny drank too much happy juice and that's how he died?" I asked, the exact order of events still a little fuzzy.

George nodded. "Like I said, I saw the whole thing. He was taking a breather after doing the horizontal mambo with one of those young hounds."

I wondered why a human would dance the mambo with a dog, but then stranger things have happened, so I let it slide. "And then what happened?"

"Well, the whippersnapper decided to go to bed and Johnny said he'd join him in just a minute. And that's when he took another one of his happy juice potions. He needed those to keep up with the young 'uns, see?" The recollection seemed to affect the big cat powerfully, for suddenly his whiskers started trembling violently. "He knocked back that juice, standing at the edge of the pool, and looking as happy as I'd ever seen him."

"Hence the name 'happy juice,'" I supplied.

"Exactly. But then, suddenly, he gasped and clutched for his heart."

"And then what happened?" asked Dooley, his own eyes also widening.

George shrugged. "He stiffened and pitched over into the pool."

"That must have been a real shock," said Dooley, hanging on the big cat's every word.

"You can bet your whiskers it was. And I would have gone in after him, but I can't swim. And I hate water. So I started screaming for help, but no one ever came. And that's when I knew Johnny was a goner."

"He drank his final happy juice," Dooley supplied, quite unnecessarily.

George sighed. "Yes, he certainly did."

"What about the boyfriend?" I asked. "Was he there when it happened?"

I already knew the answer to that one, of course, but it never hurt to double-check with an actual eyewitness.

"No, Jasper left in a huff after he made a fuss about the happy juice. And about those young hounds Johnny insisted on having over night after night."

I could definitely relate. I didn't like young hounds either, or any kind of hounds, for that matter. Dumb mutts. What surprised me was that I hadn't seen a trace of these young hounds anywhere. Looked like they'd all fled.

"Though Jasper hating those young hounds was pretty ironic," said George. "Seeing as that's how he and Johnny met in the first place."

"Because of the hounds?" I asked, confused.

"Well, he was one of them, wasn't he?"

This surprised me. A dog turning into a human was a feat I'd never seen performed. But then there are many things in this world that are beyond my comprehension. Live and learn. "He was a young hound himself once?"

"He sure was. One of the first. He was Johnny's first favorite, the one he asked to stay the night, and the night after that, and then the next night. And finally he never left, did he? Only Johnny had an insatiable appetite."

"For… hounds?" I asked.

"Sure. Jasper never had a chance of scratching that itch all by himself. Johnny needed more, and he needed different, and he needed it every single night. It drove Jasper up the wall. They fought about it all the time."

"About the happy juice and those… hounds," I said, just to be sure.

"Us cats rooted for Jasper, of course."

"Of course," I said, though how a cat could root for a dog was beyond me.

"But he never had a chance. He wanted Johnny all for himself, you see. Had visions of the two of them growing old together. But Johnny didn't do old. He wanted to stay young forever, and sharing his bed with those young studs every night made him feel young. That and the happy juice, of course."

"Young… studs," I said uncertainly. How we'd gone from dogs to horses I didn't know, but I was determined not to show my confusion.

"And of course Johnny was a star. You can't tie down a star."

Or a stud, apparently, though it's been known to happen.

"Johnny was larger than life, and nobody was going to have him all to themselves, not even me," he said with a sad look in his eyes as he silently surveyed the long row of bowls.

I got his drift, of course. Poor cat. He'd come all the way from England to America, only to have to share his human and his home with at least a dozen strays, a couple of hounds and a few studs, too. An entire menagerie, in fact.

"What's going to happen now?" I asked, gesturing at the bowls.

"Life goes on, partner. Someone will take care of us. Probably Jasper."

That figured. The dog-turned-human would take care of his cat friends. And probably kick out the hounds and studs. Almost like a Disney movie.

"You think Jasper will inherit?"

"I hope so," said George, now trying to lick his butt but finally giving up. His large belly was in the way, and he was not as limber as he used to be.

"Well, at least you'll always have Jasper," I said.

"Yeah, Jasper is a sweetheart," said George. "We're in good hands."

At this, he gave up on the struggle to lick his butt, plunked down on the floor and promptly dozed off. It happens, especially to cats of a certain age.

Dooley and I exchanged a glance, and before I could help it, I was staring wistfully at George's jumbo-sized bowl. What I would give for a helping of that delicious pâté. Just the smell was enough to make my mouth water.

"Take a nibble, Max," Dooley said. "There's plenty more where that came from. Didn't you hear the cat? They're in good hands with this Jasper."

"I am kinda peckish," I admitted. I hadn't eaten since breakfast, and after all this tripping around and interviewing cats, I could do with a bit of food.

"Well, then?" he asked. "What are you waiting for? Dig in!"

I'm not proud of what happened next. I caved. I checked left and right, like a regular bandit, and finally dug in. I was smart about it, though. Instead of cleaning out a single bowl, like Dooley had done, I simply sampled some food from all the bowls, twelve in a row, so no one would even notice. And when I'd finally reached the last one, I'd eaten my fill and was in cat heaven.

"Oh, God. This stuff is simply divine," I gushed.

"Isn't it?" asked Dooley with a grin.

"Best food I've ever tasted. Pity Odelia is not an aging pop star."

"If she was, we'd have to share with a dozen other cats," said Dooley.

He had a point. Now already we were having trouble with Brutus, the new cat in town. I couldn't imagine having to share my food and home with a dozen more like him. Or a bunch of dogs and horses, for that matter.

No, perhaps things were the way they should be. But next time when Odelia went grocery shopping, I think I'll still ask her to buy a bit of pâté.

## CHAPTER 5

We rode back to Hampton Cove in silence, Dooley and I fully content after our culinary feast. We'd told the whole story about the cats and the dogs and the horses and the happy juice to Odelia, and it was obvious we'd given her plenty of food for thought, for she was also conspicuously silent.

On our way into town, she dropped us off at the police station. Even though her uncle doesn't mind her lending a hand with the investigation, he draws the line at allowing her to sit in on interviews with suspects. But since nobody notices a couple of cats skulking about, we were her eyes and ears.

The moment we arrived, we quickly made our way to the back of the police station, where we knew Chief Alec's office was, and hopped up onto the windowsill to await further developments. The chief had just arrived back when we got there, and Chase Kingsley was in his office to discuss the case.

"Don't you think the Chief suspects we're spying on him?" asked Dooley.

"I'm sure he does. But as long as Odelia is careful how she words her articles, he's fine with it. It's Chase we have to watch out for, though. He doesn't know about Odelia's special gift, and should never find out."

"He won't find out from me," said Dooley. "Let's just hope he doesn't find out from Harriet." He gave me a knowing look.

Harriet might spill the beans to Brutus, who might try and get word out to Chase. Luckily for us he didn't share our gift of being able to talk to his human. And for Odelia's sake, it was important he never would.

Just when we arrived, Chase and the Chief packed up their files and filed out of the office, probably to continue their business in some other part of the station house. No matter. Every room had a window, and windows had sills, so... We quickly trudged over to interrogation room number one, for I had a hunch they were going to interview their first suspect. And... bingo. As we made ourselves comfortable, the Chief and Chase took a seat in front of an olive-skinned man with slicked-back black hair and dark eyes. He looked a little disheveled, and suddenly I recognized him as the man who'd been slumped over the wheel of his car. This was none other than Jasper Pruce.

"It's the boyfriend," Dooley whispered excitedly, having come to the same conclusion.

"Looks like he's been arrested," I whispered back, gesturing at his handcuffs.

"Oh, no!" cried Dooley. "That means George has no one to take care of him!"

"I'm sure Johnny had plenty of servants," I assured him. "Someone will keep that pâté coming."

Inside the room, JPG's boyfriend didn't look too happy. Upon closer inspection I could see that his eyes were blood-shot, his face haggard and his general appearance bedraggled.

He looked like a guy who'd slept in his clothes after a vicious fight, and had just discovered his boyfriend dead.

"There's only one thing I want to know from you," Chase said, opening proceedings. "And that's why you did it."

"Did what?" asked Jasper wearily.

"Don't play dumb with me," Chase growled. "We found your fingerprints on the vial containing the venom."

This made Jasper sit up and take notice, and us, too. Venom?

"What venom?" Jasper asked. "What are you talking about?"

"Don't play games, Jasper," said the Chief. "You know as well as we do you poisoned one of Johnny's GHB vials. We don't know what venom you used, exactly, but that's only a matter of time. Just tell us why you did it."

"Oh, God," said Jasper, burying his face in his hands. "Oh, no."

"Oh, yes," said Chase. "And since we only found two fingerprints on the vial: yours and Johnny's, it's obvious you planted the venom. Why did you do it, Jasper? Huh? Was it the money? Or were you simply so fed up with the endless nightly parade of young studs that you couldn't stand it anymore?"

Good thing that Odelia had patiently explained that Jasper was, in fact, human, and that the hounds and studs George had mentioned were also humans. I had to admit it was all very confusing, and I had to strain my brain to keep up. I focused on the conversation inside, and the effort must have shown on my face, for suddenly a voice sounded from the other window.

"What's wrong, Max? Chase's questions too tough for you to figure out?"

Both Dooley and I looked over, alarmed, and when we saw that Brutus sat perched on the next window, together

39

with Harriet, we almost fell from our own windowsill in shock and surprise.

"Brutus!" I cried.

"Harriet!" Dooley exclaimed.

"What are you doing here?" we both asked in unison.

The buff black cat shrugged. "Same thing you dumbbells are doing. Conducting an investigation into the murder of the warbler." He grinned. "And this time I'm going to beat you. I'm going to catch the killer and tell Chase."

"You keep forgetting you can't talk to your human," I reminded him.

His smirk disappeared. "Don't you worry about that. I'll find a way."

"You can't do this," said Dooley. "You can't take over this investigation."

"Watch me. I'm a cop cat, remember? You're just a bunch of amateurs."

My eyes swiveled to Harriet, who hadn't spoken. "How could you?"

"Yeah, how could you, Harriet?" Dooley asked, sounding even more upset than I was. He'd always had a thing for the snowy white Persian.

"I think Brutus is right," she said, lifting her chin. "I just don't think it's fair of you to give Odelia this advantage. Someone has to level the playing field, and I think Brutus is just the cat to do it. How else is Chase ever going to succeed in this town?"

"You never had any qualms about helping Odelia before," I pointed out.

"That was before." She gazed at Brutus lovingly. "Before Brutus arrived."

"Look, Chase is the one with the unfair advantage," I said. "He's the cop."

"Yeah, it's Odelia who needs all the help she can get," Dooley said.

"Odelia is not a cop," Brutus said. "So she shouldn't even be involved."

Again with his narrow-mindedness, I thought, and returned my attention to the conversation inside. It was almost as if Brutus was simply trying to distract us. "Don't listen to him, Dooley," I said. "Just ignore them both."

"Look," Chase was saying, "we know you were fed up with the constant stream of escorts, night after night. You wanted Johnny all for yourself, but you couldn't have him. So you worried that very soon Johnny would pick one of the newer, younger models over you, and kick you to the curb and that would be the end of the line for you. At forty-three you're too old for the boy toy business, and you don't have any other marketable skills to sell. So you decided that if you were ever going to cash in it had to be now, before you were pushed out. So you killed Johnny, knowing you'd be set for life."

Jasper was shaking his head throughout. "I would never hurt Johnny. I loved him!"

"We talked to his lawyer," said Chief Alec. "He confirmed that Johnny made sure that even after he died you would be taken care of. He left you the house and enough money to live out your life in luxury, enjoying the kind of lifestyle you've grown accustomed to."

"I don't care about all of that!" Jasper cried wildly. "All I cared about was Johnny!" His face took on a pleading expression. "I'm not a murderer, Chief. I would never do that."

"So why are your fingerprints on the vial?" asked Chase. "Explain that."

"I can't. But I never touched that vial, I swear. I hated those drugs. But Johnny was addicted to them. Night after night he needed his fix."

41

"And you got into a huge fight about it last night," said the Chief.

"And not for the first time, either," added Chase.

"Of course I fought Johnny on that. I could see what that stuff was doing to him. How it was turning him into a shadow of the man he used to be. His career floundered. He hadn't written a note of music in years, and couldn't even carry a tune anymore. He'd completely lost the command of his voice. That angelic voice of his had been reduced to a hoarse whisper."

Chase exchanged a grim-faced look with the Chief. "You saw the destruction and you knew it was only a matter of time before he overdosed, so you decided to speed things up before he took in another lover."

"Why would I do that? I loved Johnny! I wanted him alive and well and making music again! The last thing I wanted was for him to overdose or to die from taking that horrible stuff." Then something seemed to dawn on him. "Wait, are you telling me he didn't die from an overdose?"

"He was poisoned," the Chief confirmed. "Some exotic kind of venom administered in the vial containing GHB. Which had your fingerprints on it."

"So how did you do it?" asked Chase. "Where did you get the venom?"

"I told you, I didn't do it," said Jasper, rattling his cuffs helplessly.

"Then who did?" asked the Chief.

Jasper stared up at him. "I think I have a pretty good idea."

Dooley and I both pricked up our ears, and so did Brutus and Harriet.

Jasper leaned in. "One of the boys kept coming back. He'd quickly become one of Johnny's favorites. And obviously had high hopes to replace me in Johnny's heart. But Johnny didn't care about him. All he wanted from him was the physical satisfaction he could provide and then send him on his way. The guy obviously didn't like this. He wanted more. He wanted it all."

"Who was he?" asked the Chief.

"His name is Chico Fetcher. He was with Johnny last night. After all the other boys had left, he was still with him." He shook his head. "He's crazy. He would get high on G but it would have the worst possible effect on him. Made him go nuts. He once jumped from the roof straight into the pool. I'm sure that if anyone killed Johnny it must have been him." He looked up, tears in his eyes. "I tried to warn Johnny so many times. Even last night. I told him he should stop welcoming these people into our home, but he got mad."

"And kicked you out."

"No, never," said Jasper angrily. "I left, because I couldn't stand seeing Johnny destroy himself. Or be destroyed. And now it's too late. He's dead."

"This Chico…" said the Chief, checking his notebook.

"He's the guy who jumped out of the window," Chase said. "Probably thought he could fly."

"Did we bring him in for questioning?"

"We did. He's next door."

Chase rose and pointed an accusatory finger at Jasper. "This doesn't mean you're off the hook, Jasper."

He gave him a pained look. "I know it doesn't. I'm in hell now."

# CHAPTER 6

*a*fter Odelia had dropped off Max and Dooley, she decided to go and have a little chat with her dad. Her uncle had already messaged her the coroner's preliminary report: John Paul George had been killed by a vial of GHB that was poisoned. That, in conjunction with a preexisting heart condition, had caused his ticker to throw in the towel. Uncle Alec and Chase thought Jasper Pruce was the obvious suspect, but she decided to follow a different lead.

If a vial of Liquid G had killed Johnny, she was going to find out where that vial had come from, and who had tampered with it. Only one vial had been spiked with venom, and it was the only one that had carried a pink seal with a tiny unicorn. Johnny's seal. So the killer must have known about this.

There were no puncture marks found on the seal, so the venom hadn't been injected into the vial. Which meant it had been added before being sealed. And who else could have done that other than Johnny's dealer?

She parked her Ford pickup in front of the doctor's office and went inside. As usual, her grandmother was at the reception desk, a few patients patiently waiting until Odelia's dad, who was the town doctor, was ready.

"I need to speak to Dad," she told Gran. "It's urgent."

Gran, a wizened old lady, seemed annoyed Odelia had interrupted her game of online Scrabble. "What's this about?"

"There's been a murder," she told her. "John Paul George was found murdered in his pool this morning." She didn't mention she'd found him there, as she didn't want to make the old lady worry too much.

"The singer?" asked Gran. "Ooh, I liked him. He was a regular hottie."

Odelia's mind flashed back to the spreading man they'd dragged from the pool, and decided to skip this little bit of information too. No need to spoil Gran's memory of the eighties heartthrob. "Yeah, he was, wasn't he?"

"And you're telling me he was murdered? That's just awful! Who could have done such a horrible thing?"

"Well, that's what I'm trying to find out."

"And you think your dad knows who did it, huh?"

"I doubt it, but he might lead me in the right direction." She didn't want to put all of her cards on the table, as Gran was an inveterate gossip.

"Is that nice Detective Chase Kingsley on the case again?"

"Yes, he is."

For some reason Gran had taken a shine to Chase.

"That man is so hot, I can't believe no one has bagged him yet," she said, shooting her a meaningful look.

"Why don't you give it a shot?"

"I wouldn't want to steal your thunder, honey," said Gran. "I know that man has got the hots for you. So why haven't you made a move on him yet?"

She rolled her eyes. She was so not having this conversation right now. "I'm sure that Detective Kingsley doesn't even like me, Gran, much less wants to pursue me."

"Pursue you? What is this? A Jane Austin novel? I may be old, honey, but I'm not that old. Nowadays girls can pursue boys, you know. Trust me, if I'd waited for your grandfather to 'pursue me' I'd still be waiting. No, you go and get that man before someone else snaps him up." She gave her a wink. "Or before *I* snap him up, if you know what I mean."

"Yes, I know what you mean, Gran. It's pretty obvious." And distasteful. "Look, both Detective Kingsley and I are professionals, and we like to keep our relationship on a strictly professional level. We work together occasionally and getting… involved would only make things complicated."

Even though Chase still resented a reporter butting in on his investigation, they'd actually cracked a case together a couple of weeks ago, and even this morning, when she'd saved him from that cockatoo, there had been a sense of kinship between them. Strictly professional kinship, that was.

Gran shook her head. "Youth is definitely wasted on the young, take it from me. If I were you—"

"Well, you're not. Now if you could just tell Dad I'm here…"

"I'm giving you dibs on that hottie, but I'm not going to be able to hold back much longer, you hear?" asked Gran while she picked up the phone. "And I'm only giving you first shot because you're family."

"Thanks, Gran. That's very generous of you."

"And don't you give me that professional relationship bull, either. I know you've got the hots for that guy. I've seen the way you look at him. I may be old but there's nothing wrong with my eyesight."

"Just… give me Dad," she said through gritted teeth, and snatched the phone from her grandmother's hands. "Yes, hi, Dad. I need to ask you something real quick. Can I come in?"

And as she went in, Gran gave her a wink. "When you see

him, say hi to Chase from me, will you? Just to make sure he knows I'm still in the running, in case you drop out of the race."

"Sure, Gran. I'll tell him my grandmother is lusting after him."

"And tell him to keep up the workouts. I like my buns nice and tight."

She entered her dad's office and nodded a greeting to Mrs. Baumgartner. The old lady was in all the time, more out of habit than because something was ailing her. Her father quickly took her into the next examination room. "Make it quick, honey," he said, taking off his glasses and polishing them. "Mrs. Baumgartner was just about to show me her bunion."

In a few words she told him what had happened to Johnny.

He shook his head. "I warned him about this. Overdose, huh?"

"No, it looks like he was poisoned. At least according to the coroner."

Her dad's eyes widened. "Murder? That's terrible. He was such a great guy. Very down to earth and with a great sense of humor, too."

"So you knew him?"

"Well, he had his regular physician, a concierge doctor working out of Southampton, but I sometimes covered for him when he was on vacation. I know his boyfriend a lot better, of course. Jasper used to be my patient for years, before he started to go to Johnny's physician. Great kid, Jasper."

"Uncle Alec actually thinks Jasper might have done it. His fingerprints were on the vial of GHB that Johnny took. The one containing the venom."

"Impossible," said her dad, shaking his head decidedly.

"Jasper wouldn't hurt a fly. Besides, he loved that man dearly. They were a lovely couple."

It cemented her decision to look beyond Jasper and try to find who else might have had access to the vial and might have doctored it. "Dad, this is important. Do you have any idea who Johnny's supplier of GHB was?"

Dad gave her a look of surprise. "How on earth would I know that? I'm a doctor, not a drug dealer, honey."

"No, but you're…" She hesitated, gesturing at the medicine cabinet in a corner of the room. "Plugged in."

He laughed. "I see. You think we're all in the same business, huh?"

"Well… I just thought you might have heard something."

He thought for a moment. "There have been a lot of rumors swirling around about that health food store that opened at the mall a couple of months ago. People talk, you know, and I've been told by several of my patients that the owner of that store supplies his customers with more than just herbs and vitamins, if you catch my drift. In fact I think I saw his van pull up at Johnny's place just when I was leaving last month. Coincidence?"

She gave him a quick peck on the cheek. "Thanks, Dad. You're the best."

"So sad about Johnny," he said as they walked back into his office. "He was a very sweet man. You find out who did this, all right?"

"I will, Dad," she said.

"Oh, and be careful," he said. "This drug thing is a nasty business."

That was true enough. It had already claimed the life of one man and had landed another man in jail, possibly innocent. A very nasty business indeed.

# CHAPTER 7

*A*fter sitting in on a few interviews, Dooley and I'd had enough, so we hopped down from the windowsill and made to leave. Brutus, who had been an attentive guest throughout, along with Harriet, seemed to find our retreat funny, for he scoffed, "Leaving already, boys? Talk about lack of stamina!"

"We know when we've seen it all," I said.

"Well, I'm sticking around," he announced. "It's only starting to get good." And he returned his attention to the room behind the window, where Chase was interviewing one of what seemed like hundreds of escorts Johnny had gone through in the weeks leading up to his death. You could say whatever you wanted about the guy, but not that he didn't have the stamina Brutus was referring to. In spite of his age, he'd been up all night every night, partying like there was no tomorrow and entertaining up to a dozen men.

"I wonder how much of his behavior was Johnny and how much the drugs he took," I said as we started toward the patch of lawn in front of the police station. An American flag waved over a small plaque reminding Hampton Cove that here resided the long arm of the law. Though Uncle Alec's arms weren't really all that long, he was doing a great job interviewing a long line of witnesses testifying to Johnny's daily and nightly habits. It was obvious that the so-called recluse hadn't been all that reclusive after all.

"I think it was the drugs," said Dooley. "No man can be that voracious and that..." He struggled to find the right word.

"Enduring?" I supplied.

"Yeah. It's almost a miracle how enduring the guy was."

"I think the right word is addicted. The guy was simply addicted to sex."

"Sex, drugs and rock and roll. Talk about a walking cliché."

We padded along the sidewalk, wondering where to go from there. Chief Alec and Chase had interviewed dozens of young men and the picture of Johnny that emerged was clear: each day he'd call the agency to send him a selection of boys, all sharing the same traits. They had to be young, handsome and buff. The agency would make a selection and send over a dozen candidates. The first part of the evening would consist of Johnny entertaining them with his old video clips displayed on a big screen, and there would be lots of drinking and eating going on. As a dessert, drugs would be passed around like candy. They'd smoke pot, get high on coke and G, and things would heat up considerably. By the time midnight rolled around, the scene would look like something straight out of Caligula. The long version.

At some point Johnny would pick the boy whose exploits had impressed him the most, and invite him up to his room to spend the night. Throughout these wild parties there would be no trace of Jasper, either because he'd refuse to leave his private quarters—apparently Johnny and Jasper occupied separate wings—or he'd have stormed off after yet another row with Johnny.

Chico Fletcher, boy toy of the month, hadn't noticed anything out of the ordinary last night. But then he'd been pretty high on illegal substances. He also didn't have a motive to harm Johnny, especially seeing as he'd been hoping to replace Jasper as Johnny's new queen. You can't become queen of a dead man, so Chico was very disappointed with the way things had turned out. All he had to show for his efforts were the exorbitant fees he'd been paid.

So far the only one with an obvious motive was still Jasper, who remained firmly in the picture as the most likely suspect in the murder.

"So who do you think did it?" I asked Dooley.

"The butler, of course," said Dooley, then laughed loudly at his own joke.

"Hey, you guys!" suddenly a voice sounded behind us. "Wait up!"

She sounded a lite out of breath, as if she'd been running, and when we both turned in surprise, we saw we'd been joined by none other than Harriet.

I checked around, but could see no trace of Brutus. "Where's your boyfriend?" I asked.

She made a gesture with her tail. "Still glued to the police station window." She rolled her eyes. "If I have to listen to one more boy toy talking about how hot and sexy John Paul George was I'm going to be sick."

We walked along the pavement together, and Dooley asked, "So how's Brutus's investigation going?"

"Very well, thank you, Dooley. I think Brutus has a definite lead on the killer, and it won't be long before he shares his observations with Chase."

I gave her a sideways glance. "You do know that Brutus can't talk to his owner, right?"

"Of course I know, silly," she said. "But he's promised me he'll fix that."

"By using sign language?" I asked. "No, seriously though. How does he hope to find the killer and help the investigation? He's a policeman's cat, not a police cat. There's a difference."

That was the rub right there: just because you were the cat of a policeman that didn't magically transfer the man's sleuthing powers to you. Dooley and I had been doing this with Odelia for a very long time, so we knew how to proceed. Brutus was a complete newbie at this sleuthing business, though, and I'm sure that Harriet knew this but was too proud to admit it.

"Hey, I know what you're doing," said Dooley now.

"I'm walking along the street with my friends, that's what I'm doing," said Harriet.

"No, you're not. You're spying on us. Brutus doesn't know which way to turn so he instructed you to spy on us and hope to find out what we know."

"That's just ridiculous," she said primly. "You know as well as I do that all I want is for us to be friends, just like in the old days."

"Only that will never happen if you keep hanging out with Brutus," I said.

"Oh, God, you're being melodramatic again, you two," said Harriet. "Can't you simply accept that Brutus is part of the gang now?"

"Never," I said adamantly.

"No way," Dooley agreed.

"You guys," she said, sounding exasperated, "Brutus is a really nice cat, once you get to know him. In fact he's just great. He's strong and generous and sweet and caring… He's a great friend. He really is."

"A friend who likes to tell us what to do, where to go, who we can and cannot meet? That doesn't sound like a nice cat to me. More like a despot."

"Brutus is simply set in his ways," Harriet argued. "I'm sure that if you give him time, he'll come around to the way we do things around here. You have to remember he's a big city cat, and they do things different over there."

"Oh, I'll say they do," said Dooley.

We walked on in silence for a moment. Even in spite of Harriet's recent betrayal, it still felt good to be just the three of us again, just like old times, and I could sense that Dooley, too, was secretly glad that Harriet was trying to be our friend again. This whole Brutus business had hit him hard.

"So what do we do now?" asked Harriet. "What's our next move?"

Dooley's eyebrows rose at her use of the term 'we'. "We were just going over to the general store, to see what the word on the street is," he said.

"Yeah, we wanted to pick Kingman's brain. See what he has to say."

Kingman was the cat of Wilbur Vickery, owner of Vickery General Store on Main Street, and a great source of information on what was happening in this town and what people were talking about. Along with the barbershop and the doctor's office, the store was among our favorite places to hang out.

Kingman slept all day on Wilbur's counter, and even though it looked like he was out of it, he was actually acutely aware of everything that went on around him, which made him such a great source of information.

"Good idea," said Harriet cheerfully. "Let's go talk to Kingman."

I had my qualms about Harriet being an agent for the enemy, like Dooley had said, but decided to let her tag along anyway. It would have been sad to have to send her away, especially as she'd been our friend for as long as the three of us had been alive on this planet. I guess I was just being sentimental.

## CHAPTER 8

We arrived at the general store, and walked straight in through the open door. As usual, Kingman was asleep on his high perch on the counter, while Wilbur was busily ringing up his customers.

"Psst, hey, Kingman," I said.

The spreading piebald opened one lazy eye and stared down at us, then acknowledged our presence by grunting, "Meet me outside in five."

We did as we were told and trooped out again, staking out a spot next to the display table full of fruits and vegetables. Five minutes later, Kingman came trotting out. "Wilbur doesn't like it when the place is full of cats," he said, quite surprisingly.

"Why?" I asked. "He's never had a problem with cats before."

"There's been a spate of thefts lately," said Kingman, "and he suspects cats are involved. I've been trying to catch them but they're pretty sneaky."

"Well, we would never steal anything," said Dooley.

"You stole an entire bowl of pâté this morning," I reminded him.

"That was different."

"How was that different? You cleaned out Princess's bowl. I saw you."

"Princess? Who's Princess?" asked Harriet.

"Just some cat," said Dooley vaguely.

"John Paul George's cat."

"And you cleaned out her bowl?" asked Harriet.

"We were guests," said Dooley. "Guests are allowed to eat a host's food."

"Not when you're not invited, you're not," I said.

"We were invited."

"How were we invited? The host was dead. You can't be invited by a dead host."

Dooley rolled his eyes. "Oh, please. You ate from all the bowls."

I shrugged. "I was hungry. If I don't eat I get cranky."

"All right, all right, all right," said Kingman now. "Settle down, you guys. It's not stealing if the food's out there in the open, all right?"

"See?" asked Dooley. "I wasn't stealing. I was just sampling."

"An entire bowl?" I asked. "That's not sampling. That's gobbling."

"Who's Princess?" Harriet asked again. "Have I met her?"

"No, you haven't," I said. "She's one of Johnny's dozen cats."

Harriet gave Dooley a curious look. "So why did you eat her food?"

"It was pâté, all right?" cried Dooley. "I couldn't resist."

"Actual pâté?" asked Kingman, interested.

"Yeah, the expensive kind," Dooley said. "To die for, I swear."

"It was pretty good," I conceded.

"Pretty good? It was the best food I've ever tasted."

"So what does this Princess look like?" asked Harriet.

"Can we just talk about the dead guy now?" I asked. I was already regretting having started this whole thing about the pâté. If you're going to accuse someone of stealing, you better make sure you haven't stolen the stuff yourself, I now discovered. It kinda destroys your moral superiority.

"Yeah, what about that, huh?" asked Kingman with a shake of the head. "A regular murder in Hampton Cove. What's the world coming to?"

"So you heard about that?" asked Dooley. He shouldn't have been surprised. Kingman always knew everything that was going on in this town.

"The mayor's wife came in early this morning to buy plums to make plum pie, and she'd heard it from her husband who'd heard it from the Chief that the body of John Paul George was found floating face down in his pool."

"News sure travels fast," said Harriet, still studying Dooley.

"It sure does," said Kingman with a grin. Like most cats in Hampton Cove he had a thing for Harriet, who was pretty much the prettiest cat for miles around. Except for Princess, maybe, which was probably why Harriet was so curious to find out more about her. Keep an eye on the competition.

"Any idea who did it?" asked Dooley.

"I could ask you the same thing. You were out there, weren't you? One of Johnny's cats strolled by here before. Said you were all over their place."

"We only know what we saw," said Dooley. "JPG in the pool. Poisoned."

I gave him a warning look. Even though the story about Johnny's death by poisoning would spread through town fast, there was no need to help it along. At least not until Odelia had written her article and got the scoop.

"Poisoned, huh?" asked Kingman, his furry face puckering up in surprise. "Now there's something I didn't know. Are you sure about this?"

Dooley stared at me and I shook my head. "Nah," he said. "We, um…"

"It's just a rumor that's going around," said Harriet, coming to his aid.

"And who do they think did it?" asked Kingman now.

"They're interviewing all the guys Johnny entertained last night," I said, "but so far it looks like the boyfriend is the most likely suspect. Jasper Pruce." I wasn't giving away any big secrets, as Jasper had been arrested.

"Who would have thought?" asked Kingman, whistling through his teeth.

Yes, cats can whistle, but we rarely do it, on account of the fact that it looks silly, and if there's anything we hate as much as we hate dogs, it's looking silly in front of other cats. We like to play it cool. Where else do you think the expression 'cool cat' comes from?

"So the boyfriend did it, huh?" asked Kingman now.

"Personally I think he's innocent," said Harriet. "He sounded extremely sincere when he said he loved Johnny and would never hurt him. And he doesn't look like a killer at all. More like a sad little kitten."

"Looks can be deceiving," said Dooley. "And so can people's words. They say one thing to your face and do something else behind your back."

Harriet lifted her chin. "Well, I for one believed him. Jasper Pruce is simply incapable of murdering the person he loved. Love is like that, you know. It makes one care about the other, in spite of their obvious flaws."

"Ah! So you admit there are flaws," said Dooley.

"No one is without flaws," said Harriet philosophically.

Well, that was true enough, but was Jasper flawed enough to have murdered his boyfriend? I didn't know, but I wasn't as gullible as Harriet to let a few tears and vows of never-ending love sway me. As far as I knew, he was the killer, even if Harriet chose to believe he was innocent.

"I think the boyfriend did it," said Kingman, giving his opinion even though nobody had asked him. "Just think about it. Isn't it always the husband or the wife that did it? So why not the boyfriend? Especially as there's big money involved this time."

"You just might be right," I said. "What do the people in town think?"

"Most of them seem to agree that Jasper did it. Just so he could get his hands on the money, and make sure he wasn't replaced by a younger model before he did. That endless parade of pretty young boys must have rubbed him the wrong way," said Kingman, and that seemed to be the consensus.

"I think it's sad," said Harriet.

"What's sad?" asked Kingman. "That Jasper killed him for his money?"

"That people have so little faith in the words of a man who was in love, and remained by Johnny's side in this, the aging pop star's twilight years."

"Johnny wasn't that old," Kingman said.

"You know what I mean. It's obvious that Jasper loved Johnny very much, to stay with him and have to watch how he threw his life away." She sighed. "But then that's true love for you. You simply stick together through the good and the bad, in sickness and in health, until death do you part." She wiped away a tear. "I think it's all so very, very romantic. And so very sad."

"Yeah, yeah," said Dooley, holding up his paw. "I think I've heard enough. You love Brutus and he loves you and there's nothing we can do."

"Nice rhyming skills, bro," said Kingman.

"I was talking about you, you fool," Harriet suddenly burst out, giving Dooley a thump on the shoulder. "You don't desert a friend just because they happen to fall in love. Real friends stick together, through thick and thin."

At this, she promptly turned around and stalked off, her nose in the air, leaving both Dooley and I stunned on the sidewalk. Kingman, though, laughed loudly. "Trouble in paradise, boys? What was all that about?"

I decided not to elaborate, as otherwise the story of this outburst would soon travel the entire town. Not that there was a lot we could do to stop that. Kingman would make sure that everyone knew that Dooley, Harriet and I had had a very public falling-out. And all because of that brute Brutus.

"What was Harriet talking about?" asked Dooley after we'd said goodbye to Kingman, promising to keep him in the loop.

"I have absolutely no idea," I said, though perhaps this breaking up of the band had hit Harriet more than she let on. Being forced to choose between your best friends and your boyfriend must be a tough proposition, and it was obvious that Harriet wasn't taking it well.

"Maybe we should make friends with Brutus," Dooley said now.

"Never," I told him adamantly. "That cat is the worst thing that has ever happened to this town, and we can't let him think he's defeated us."

"But why can't we simply try to get along?" asked Dooley.

I knew that the only reason he wanted to extend the olive branch was so he could get Harriet back into our lives.

I stopped mid-stride. "Look, Brutus is the enemy of

everything we hold dear. If we let him, he will turn Hampton Cove into a prison camp."

"I think you're exaggerating, Max. I think deep down he's not such a bad cat. He's just... socially awkward."

This was just too much. "You mean like Hitler was socially awkward? Or Stalin? That cat is the enemy, Dooley, and don't you forget it!"

Dooley stared at me. "But I miss her, Max. I miss having Harriet around."

"Well, that's her choice. If she wants to hang with that cat and not with us, tough luck."

"Tough luck for me," said Dooley moodily.

"Look, I don't like this situation either," I told him. "I like Harriet and I miss her. But if we don't stand firm on this, it's the end of life as we know it."

"Yeah, yeah, yeah," he muttered.

It was obvious he was weakening. In the fight against the enemy, the enemy was winning crucial points. If even my best friend was already thinking about throwing in the towel, things were looking very glum indeed. I gave Dooley a gentle tap on the shoulder. "Hey. Don't look so glum, chum."

"I look glum because I feel glum," he said glumly.

"Look, we'll solve this murder and show Brutus he's not the boss of us. Maybe then he'll admit he was wrong to try and bully us into submission."

"You think so?" Dooley asked, looking a little less glum.

"Of course. It works both ways. Harriet might be sent by Brutus to convince us to play ball, but two can play that game. We can use our influence on Harriet to convince Brutus he's the one that should change."

"I like that," said Dooley softly.

I liked it, too. Though I doubted very much if Brutus was the kind of cat that could be persuaded to change his tune. Some cats simply never change.

# CHAPTER 9

*O*delia parked her aged, old pickup in front of the health food store. She'd been there a couple of times. Though she wasn't big on health food solutions, she had been taking her daily vitamins lately, hoping they would give her the advertised energy boost. Her mom was the bigger fan, and Gran, too. Every time Odelia was over at her parents' place she saw how her mom and grandma popped the herbal capsules by the dozen, probably hoping to extend their life-span or to cure some disease they hadn't yet contracted.

She entered the store and for a moment spent some time perusing the displays and the shelves stocked full. From fat reducing pills to stuff guaranteed to boost the immune system, she was sure her mom had tried them all. She picked up a box of capsules that promised to add extra Omega-3 fatty acids to her diet and reduce joint pain, and walked up to the counter at the back of the store. A man with a hipster beard and horn-rimmed glasses greeted her with a jovial smile. "Found something, hon?"

"I, um…" She wondered how to launch into a line of

questioning that would lead the man to confess he was JPG's drug supplier, and placed the box on the counter. "I found these," she said with a fake grin. How easy it would be if she could just get Uncle Alec to let her flash a fake police badge. People answered all kinds of questions when they thought you were a cop.

"If you buy a second item today it's fifty percent off," said the guy.

"Actually I was wondering if you have something a little stronger?"

He eyed her over his glasses for a moment. "Stronger than Omega-3? What about the Omega-3-6-9 complex? More bang for your buck."

She quickly checked left and right, making a display of trying to be discreet. Inadvertently the man moved a little closer. "I'm having a hard time relaxing at night," she said. "And it's taken a toll on my..." She felt a blush creep up her cheeks. "On my love life," she finally whispered.

A smile now spread across the man's face, although it was hard to see through that bushy beard. "You need something to boost your love life?"

"Yeah, something really powerful," she said. "Something... awesome."

He nodded. "I've got exactly what you need right here." He rummaged around beneath the counter for a moment, and Odelia's heart skipped a beat.

Now she was getting somewhere. But instead of vials of GHB, he carefully placed a small box on the counter. She leaned in and saw that it said, 'Firm Up Your Sex Life with Ginseng—Bedroom Miracle Cure.'

"How about that, huh?" the salesman asked. "That should hit the spot."

"I..." She gestured at the ginseng. "Is that the best you can do? I mean," she corrected herself, "Is that the most potent stuff in the store?"

"Sure is, hon. And all yours for nineteen-ninety-nine. Real bargain. Before you know it, you and your boyfriend will be humping like rabbits." When she glared at him, he quickly corrected, "Or you and your girlfriend?"

She probably shouldn't have mentioned her non-existent love life, but that didn't give this guy the right to become personal. "Look, buster," she said, running out of patience with this oversized bearded hobbit, "I know for a fact that you sell Liquid G out of this shop and don't you dare deny it."

At this, his perfectly groomed rectangular beard waggled. "Liquid G? I think you're mistaking me for someone else, honey. This is a health food store. I strictly deal in health food solutions, not drugs."

"Oh, yes, you do," suddenly a gruff voice sounded behind Odelia.

She didn't even have to turn around to know who the voice belonged to. "Why is that wherever I go you keep showing up, Detective Kingsley?"

"I could ask you the same thing, Miss Poole," he returned, then flashed his badge to the man behind the counter, who was still clutching the ginseng. "Please tell me you can do better than that," he said, gesturing at the ginseng.

The man looked horrified. "You're both cops?"

"No, Miss Poole is a reporter for the Hampton Cove Gazette. I'm with the Hampton Cove PD, Mr. Haggis. She likes to think she's a cop, though."

"I was doing great before you showed up," she snapped.

"Yeah, you were doing fantastic. So you're having issues with your love life, huh?"

"You heard that?" she asked, that blush creeping further up her cheeks.

"Even if I hadn't wanted to, it was unavoidable. Your voice carries."

"I was trying to be discreet," she said, giving him her best scowl.

"And failing miserably, as usual." He turned to the shopkeeper. "Mr. Orville Haggis, I presume? Owner and proprietor of The Vitamin King?"

"Uh-huh."

"The question still stands, Orville. Were you selling GHB to JPG?"

The man's mouth opened, then closed again, causing his beard to move as if operating on a hinge. Finally, he admitted, "Yes, I was." He sighed, closing his eyes. "You wouldn't believe how much ginseng you have to sell to make a living around here. So I have to supplement my income by shifting some of the more pricey items on the side. Johnny kept me in business."

"Now we're talking," said Chase, with a quick glance at Odelia.

"I notice you're referring to Johnny in the past tense, Mr. Haggis," she said. "So you're aware that he died last night?"

"I heard about that, yeah," said Orville. "But I swear I had nothing to do with that."

"I beg to differ," said Chase. "I think you had everything to do with that. You see, it was your product that killed Johnny."

"That's impossible," said Orville. "I always gave him the right dose. Johnny knew the deal. One vial and that's it. He knew the risks, so if he took more than one, that's not my fault."

"What is your fault is that you were delivering an illegal substance to a very unstable pop star," said Chase.

"Johnny wasn't unstable. He knew exactly what he was doing."

"Did you always deliver your vials with a seal?" asked Odelia.

"Yes, I did. The ones I prepared for Johnny carried his personal seal."

She smiled. "Pink with a unicorn, right?"

"That's right," he said. "That's the way he wanted it."

"Any way the vials could have been tampered with?" she asked.

"What do you mean?" he asked. "I thought he died from an overdose."

"Someone laced Johnny's GHB with a very potent venom," she said. "Which caused his heart to fail. Any idea what venom was used?" she asked Chase.

He stared at her, then rolled his eyes. "I shouldn't be telling you this, but since you're going to simply turn around and ask your uncle I might as well. The venom found belongs to the Australian funnel-web spider."

She stared at him. "Spider venom?"

"Not just any spider. Apparently it's the most lethal spider in the world. The weird thing? The venom is deadly only if injected directly into the bloodstream. When imbibed, its proteins are broken down by stomach acid, and the effect is greatly diminished. The only reason the venom was toxic in this case, is because Johnny was suffering from an enlarged heart, possibly caused by years of drug abuse."

"So whoever administered the venom…"

"Was a rank amateur," said Chase.

They both turned to Orville. "So it looks like you decided to off your best customer, Orville," Chase said. "Now all I want to know is where you got the venom."

"Spider venom? Are you crazy? I don't even—why would I kill my best customer?"

"If you didn't put that venom in that vial, who did?" asked Odelia.

"How should I know? I delivered the stuff to Johnny once a week. Enough vials for his guests, and the special batch I mixed up for him distinguished by the pink seal so nobody could tamper with it."

"And you're sure nobody could have had access to the vials? Someone who knew about this arrangement between you and Johnny?" she asked.

"Positive. I'm a one man operation and I personally prepared Johnny's happy juice, as he liked to call it. Between this place and Johnny's house, nobody messed with those vials. If they were tampered with, it must have been by someone at Johnny's end. Someone who knew about the pink seal."

"How easy is it to reseal those vials?" asked Odelia.

"Very easy. It's basically just a small sticker I put on top. Anybody could have peeled it off, dumped in that spider venom, and resealed it. Didn't you find any fingerprints on the vial?"

"We did," said Chase, darting a knowing look at Odelia. "Looks like we got the right man in jail after all." Then he turned back to the health food guy, plucking a pair of hand-cuffs from his belt. "Orville Haggis, you're under arrest for the illegal distribution—"

But before he could finish his sentence, Orville decided to skedaddle.

"Hey!" Chase yelled as the guy swung around and disap-peared through a door behind him. "Hell," the cop grunted, and vaulted the counter. "You wait here, Poole."

But Odelia had a better idea. She quickly raced through the store and slammed through the front door. As she did, she saw Orville straddling a red Ducati and, as she watched, kicked it to life and raced off. She ran to her pickup and hopped in. After a few coughs, the engine roared to life, and she backed the car up on screeching tires. Just then, Chase came bolting full-speed through the small alley dividing The Vitamin King from the Chinese restaurant next door. She pushed open the passenger door. "Hop in!"

And then she was stomping down on the accelerator, tires squealing and spraying the front of The Vitamin King with gravel. Finally finding purchase, the truck lurched forward and they were off at a healthy clip in pursuit of the hipster drug dealer. The pickup bumped into a depression in the asphalt at the edge of the parking lot and then swung onto the main road, merging into traffic with smoking tires.

"Please tell me you learned how to drive since the last time I rode with you," Chase said, sounding a little winded.

"Please tell me that that short chase didn't knock the wind out of you."

"I haven't found a decent fitness club in town yet," he grumbled. "It's been weeks since my last training session and I'm starting to feel the strain."

"There's a great club at that strip mall we just left," she said. "I used to go there all the time."

"So what made you stop?"

"Between work at the Gazette and the club suddenly jacking up its prices I decided I needed to buy myself an elliptical trainer and work out at home."

"And how do you like the machine? I might get one myself."

She gave him a rueful look. "Actually I haven't gotten round to buying one yet. But I will!" she quickly added when he laughed and shook his head.

Orville was setting a nice pace, and she had to focus when they reached the heart of town. Between pedestrians and traffic she had to be careful not to hit anyone, while Orville didn't have a large pickup to navigate and could easily slip through on his more flexible two-wheeler.

"Maybe I should buy a bike instead of a home trainer," she

said, cursing under her breath when she had to stop for two women crossing with strollers.

"So why don't you?"

"Three cats," she said. "They wouldn't like it if I traded in my old Ford."

"You take those cats everywhere?"

"Hey, I'm the cat lady, remember?"

"I said that one time," he grumbled.

She smiled. "I'm like an elephant. I never forget a thing."

"You don't look like an elephant." She blushed, and immediately he held up his hands. "I shouldn't have said that. I'm sorry."

"No, I take it you meant that as a compliment?"

"Yes, I did mean it as a compliment."

She gave him a quick sideways glance. The way he was sitting there, with his muscular frame stretching his shirt, his long legs clad in jeans, he looked more than fine. In fact he looked downright sexy. A hottie, Gran would say. But what was up with the compliments? That was definitely a first. Then she decided to focus on the mission at hand: capturing a known drug dealer. She could think about Chase Kingsley all she wanted when this was over.

Finally, they'd reached the road leading out of town, and she slammed down the accelerator, causing Chase to be knocked back against his seat.

"Christ, be careful, will you? I don't want to die in the line of duty yet."

"Don't worry," she said, gritting her teeth as she kept her eyes focused on the small dot in the distance that was Orville Haggis. "I'm a great driver."

"If you manage to keep us alive *and* catch the bad guy, I'll believe you."

They were on a straight strip of road now, and she ratcheted up the engine to the sticking point, going as fast as she dared to take it, and still they weren't gaining on the Ducati. But at least they weren't falling behind either.

"I better call the Chief," said Chase. "Maybe he can set up a roadblock."

"Don't call him yet," she said. "I'm going to catch Mr. Ginseng."

"Are you always so eager to catch your guy?"

"Sure. If you come into my town dealing drugs, I'm going to hunt you down." She glanced over. "We're big on civic duty in Hampton Cove."

"So I've noticed," he said. "And while I think that's admirable, you might want to leave the heroics to the trained professionals."

She smiled. "Like the trained professional who couldn't catch a hipster drug dealer?" To add emphasis to her words, she punched her foot down all the way to the floor of the car. The engine responded with a roaring whine, as if asking her to cut it out already.

"Uh-oh," said Chase. "This old thing is gonna blow."

They were finally gaining on the bearded ginseng huckster, and she now overtook him. Chase stared at Orville and Orville stared back, seemingly surprised that his great escape had been thwarted by this duo in a beat-up old Ford pickup.

Chase rolled down the window and shouted, "Pull over!"

"No way, cop!" yelled Orville.

This decided Odelia. She had no time to be chasing drug dealers while she had a murder to solve back in Hampton Cove and about a dozen articles to write. So she quickly swung the car to the right, nudging Motorcycle Man.

"Hey!" the guy yelled, but before he could react, he was on the shoulder in a plume of dust and then drove straight into the ditch.

"Oh, God," said Chase. "Now you've gone and killed a suspect."

"I didn't kill him," she said, pulling over. "I just dented him a bit."

The car came to a stop in a cloud of smoke, and they both got out to check Ginseng Guy. When they finally found him in the ditch, ten feet from his gleaming red Ducati, he was lying on his back, staring up at the sky with a startled expression on his face, as if he didn't believe how his day had gone.

The moment he caught sight of Odelia floating into his field of vision, he shouted, "You wrecked my favorite bike!"

"You wrecked my favorite pop star," she returned.

The guy shrugged. "He was always going to wreck himself. If I hadn't supplied that G, someone else would have."

"Always the same lame excuse," Chase grumbled as he outfitted the man with a nice pair of shiny handcuffs and hoisted him to his feet. "You're under arrest, buddy. And I'm confiscating your bike. What's left of it, anyway."

"See?" asked Odelia. "He's fine. Just a few bruises." Her eyes dropped to the seat of his pants where now a large hole had appeared and a pair of Minnie Mouse boxers were visible. "And some vestimentary issues."

"Oh, my God!" cried the guy when he caught sight of his own underwear sticking out. "I can't be seen like this! I have to think about my rep!"

"Don't worry. You'll have plenty of time to think about that in jail," said Chase, and gave Odelia a wink. "That was some pretty effective driving."

"Can I quote you on that, Detective?"

He laughed, flashing his dimples. Maybe Gran was right. Maybe she had to snap this guy up before some other bimbo did. Maybe. But not today.

# CHAPTER 10

*A*fter Odelia dropped off Chase and Orville at the police station, she drove to the Gazette. While in transit, Orville had intimated he might have an idea who could be responsible for this John Paul George business after all. He said another dealer had been trying to muscle in on his territory and had approached JPG several times trying to hawk his wares. He basically sold the same stuff, only a lot cheaper, and had also approached a couple of Orville's other regulars—apparently a lot of celebs liked the occasional toke.

This other dealer didn't operate from a store but sold his stuff from the trunk of his car. Orville had given Chase all the information he had, and the cop had promised he'd be on the lookout for this second dealer.

She parked in front of the Gazette, and for the next couple of hours worked diligently on her stories for tomorrow's edition. The John Paul George story was obviously the biggest one, but she had a few other smaller articles to finish before deadline. Like the recent Jeanie Fidget wedding, already the fifth attempt at marital bliss for the Oscar-winning actress, and a car crashing into the house of a super-model, pretty much wrecking the place.

And she was just finishing up an article on the upcoming town hall meeting, when Dan swung by her office. "Hey, kid. How's it going in here?"

She sat back and smiled up at the aged editor. "Just fine, Dan. I think I've got tomorrow's edition pretty much nailed down."

"The murder case?"

"Yeah, that's the big one. Front page, I guess?"

"Damn right. It's been a while since anyone of JPG's stature got whacked."

"I'm guessing someone of JPG's stature has never been whacked in this town."

"Ah, but what little do you know, young Padawan. Back in the sixties, when I was just a young whippersnapper myself, Ryland Sundry got whacked in similar fashion. Created a big hullaballoo as you can imagine."

"Whacked in similar fashion, huh? You mean Ryland Sundry's vial of GHB got laced with spider venom by his live-in lover and former escort? Because he was jealous a new boy toy had arrived on the scene?"

Dan laughed loudly. "Not exactly! Things were a little different back then, as you can imagine. No GHB and no boy toys. Though we did have escorts, but we didn't call them that, and they were a lot more discreet about their business as otherwise they would have been arrested for lewd conduct. No, actually Ryland was killed for refusing to marry his housekeeper."

"Sounds like something out of *The Bold and the Beautiful*."

"Ryland, famous in the silent film era, had an affair with his housekeeper and got her pregnant. He'd promised to take care of her and the kid but later reneged on his promise when his wife found out about the affair."

"So the housekeeper killed him?"

"Not exactly. If I recall correctly, it was actually the housekeeper's kid that did it. His illegitimate daughter. She got so mad her movie star dad abandoned her and her mother that she decided to take matters into her own hands and commit patricide. I seem to remember an icepick featured pretty prominently in the story."

"Ouch."

"Yeah. The prick deserved it, though. Or at least that was the prevailing sentiment at the time. The story dominated the front pages for months, especially after a jury acquitted the girl, and she walked free."

"Did she ever get her payday?"

"Not a chance. She did write a book, though. A real bestseller."

"I'll bet they even turned it into a movie."

"Just a Lifetime movie, but still," Dan said with a grin.

"You're right. This JPG business has echoes of that Ryland Sundry case, only I'm afraid that they've got the wrong guy in jail. I mean, why would Jasper kill his boyfriend? It's pretty obvious he loved JPG. It doesn't make sense."

"Jealousy, of course. The guy was way past his boy toy prime, honey."

"He was only forty-three."

"Exactly. I think he was afraid he'd outlasted his usefulness. Weren't he and JPG living in separate wings of that big house of theirs?"

She nodded. "Looks like."

He spread his arms. "Well, then. I'm sure it was only a matter of time before he was pushed out entirely, making space for a new beau. Guys like JPG aren't exactly known for their faithfulness. The fact that he never put a ring on Jasper's finger tells you all you need to know about that relationship."

"Maybe they had their reasons for not tying the knot?"

"Money being the biggest one," said Dan. "Mark my words, honey, if Alec thinks Jasper Pruce did it, there's a very good chance that he did. That uncle of yours is no dummy, and the new guy is no idiot either."

"We caught a drug dealer together," she said with a grin.

"Good for you. Just make sure you're careful out there."

"Always, Dan. Always."

# CHAPTER 11

*a*fter she had finished writing her articles for the day, she decided to drop by the library to have a chat with her mother. Mom usually had good ideas. And she knew a lot of people through her work at the library. She wasn't convinced that Uncle Alec had locked up the right guy, and if he thought he had, he wasn't going to look any further. She felt very strongly he should continue the investigation, but if he wasn't going to do it, she certainly was.

She walked into the library, and saw that her mother was pushing the book trolley, placing recently returned books back on their shelves.

"Hey, Mom," she said as she walked up to the woman who was like the spitting image of herself, only three decades older.

"Hey, honey," said her mother. "I hear you've been busy today?"

"Yeah, we had an actual murder case to tackle," she said as she picked up a book and placed it in its rightful place.

It didn't surprise her that her mother already knew what had happened. Sometimes she wondered why Dan even bothered to put out the Gazette, as the stories he wrote were old news by the time the paper dropped into people's mailboxes. Maybe they just wanted to see the pictures that went with the stories, or check up on some detail they might have missed.

"Is it true that the boyfriend did it?" her mother asked now.

"I don't know. Uncle Alec seems to think so but I have my doubts."

"Then that makes two of us."

"It does?" she asked, surprised.

"I've met Jasper Pruce," said her mother, "and he didn't strike me as a man capable of murder. Such a sweet young man."

"He's forty-three."

"Is he?" asked her mother. "He looks a great deal younger."

"He probably moisturizes."

"I'll bet he does. And not the cheap brands, either."

"So you met him, huh?"

"We have. He's in here all the time. He loves his romance novels," she said with a smile. "He also loves to chat, and he struck me as a very earnest and very nice man. Very concerned about his husband's health."

"They weren't married, Mom."

"Well, for all intents and purposes they were. Besides, I'm sure they would have gotten married if Johnny hadn't been married already."

Odelia frowned. "Married already? What do you mean?"

"Didn't you know? Johnny married that woman, what's her name…"

"Johnny was married… to a woman?"

"Sure." She snapped her fingers. "Bryony Pistol. Used to be his backing vocalist back in the eighties, when he was still carving out a career. They got married at some point and, at least according to Jasper, they still were."

"But why? Why didn't he divorce her?"

"Well, he did owe her his career, so maybe that's why? And they had a daughter together, of course. She must be in her late twenties now."

"A daughter!"

Mom shook her head. "And you call yourself a reporter. Yeah, Johnny pretty much owed everything to Bryony. She came from money, and supported him in the early days of his career, when he was just a struggling artist. It took him several years to break through and get his first big hit."

"*I'm Your Bi-ba-boy*. I loved that song."

Her mother stared at her dubiously. She might like Jasper, but she was obviously not a fan of Johnny's music. "Anyway, Bryony paid all the bills and basically squandered her family's fortune to make it happen for Johnny, simply because she believed in his talent so much."

"She squandered her own money?"

"All of it."

"Ouch."

"Yeah. Lucky for her the gamble paid off. Big time. Johnny became a global superstar. And then he told her he liked boys better than girls so they separated. This was the nineties, I think. I'm a little fuzzy on the details."

"How come I didn't know about this?"

"Because Johnny valued his privacy. I doubt you'll find this information anywhere. If Jasper hadn't told me, I would never have known. It was obvious the whole Bryony business didn't sit well with him, though."

"Nor would the whole Jasper business have sat well with Bryony."

Her mother held up her hands. "That, I don't know. I

never met Bryony. She's not a library person, apparently," she said with a look of distaste.

For Odelia's mother, there were only two types of people in the world: people who liked books, and people who didn't. It was obvious which kind she favored. "I wonder what Bryony thought about this whole drug thing."

"Why don't you ask her? I'm sure it's an angle your uncle Alec hasn't thought about yet. And it would make for a great article for your paper."

"You just might be right," she agreed.

"Of course I'm right."

"Now about dinner tonight. Don't be late, because we have a guest over."

She groaned. "Not Chase Kingsley again?"

"Yes, Chase Kingsley again. I really don't know what you've got against that man."

"He keeps showing up."

"Well, that's because he's a cop, dear. Cops have a habit of showing up everywhere. They wouldn't be doing their jobs if they didn't."

"But why do you insist on feeding him? I'm sure he can take care of himself."

"I doubt that. Living with Alec as he does the man would simply starve to death if he didn't get fed, and so would your uncle himself, for that matter."

"I'm sure that Alec cooks, and so does Chase."

"And I'm sure they don't," said her mother decidedly. "Now please be punctual. Dinner will be served at seven, and I expect you to be there." She frowned. "Why do I have the feeling I'm forgetting something?" Then her face cleared. "Oh, that's right. Can you bake a cake, honey? Your gran was going to, but she forgot she had bingo at the senior center this afternoon."

"Cake?" she asked. "I don't have time to bake a cake, Mom. Why don't you buy one from the general store?"

Her mother's face puckered up into an expression of distaste. "You know those aren't freshly baked, honey. They make them in some factory somewhere by mixing a bunch of chemicals and other goop. No, what we need is that chocolate cake of yours. I'm sure Chase will be impressed."

She glared at her mother. "You're trying to set me up with Chase again, aren't you? First Gran, and now you."

"I don't know what you're talking about, honey," said her mother primly. "But you could do a lot worse than Chase Kingsley. He's a nice, big, strapping young man, with a nice, secure income, a good position in this community, and I'm sure he'll make some girl a very happy bride some day so why not you?"

"His position in this community is pretty rocky right now, and if he doesn't watch his back he's going to be out of a job soon, too," she said.

Mom rolled her eyes. "Still with that horrible harassment thing?"

"Still with the horrible *molestation* thing. There's several petitions doing the rounds to have him kicked off the force. I even saw one at that health food store you like so much. The one that deals GHB under the counter."

"Well, then you'll just have to make sure those silly charges go away, won't you?" asked Mom as she plunked another large volume onto the shelf and decidedly pushed it into place. "You know as well as I do that Chase is innocent of those silly charges, and I'm sure that if you clear his name he'll be ever so grateful." She gave her a knowing glance. "And a grateful man is a marrying man, honey. Remember that."

. . .

*S*he left the library feeling a little annoyed. First her grandmother tried to push her into Chase's arms and now her mother. It was a concerted matchmaking effort that didn't sit well with her. If she was ever going to choose a mate for life, as her grandmother put it, she'd do it herself, without anyone's help. Besides, clearing Chase's name wasn't as easy as it sounded.

Back when he was still an NYPD detective, the wife of a suspect had accused him of molesting her, and those charges had lost him his job and, very briefly, his freedom. And they weren't going away. Instead, they'd followed him to Hampton Cove, where his job now hung in the balance.

Chase claimed he'd caught the NYPD commissioner and the wife of the mayor of New York in a torrid affair, and they'd set up this molestation claim to discredit him and shut him up. Since arriving in Hampton Cove, he'd apprehended the killer in another murder case, that of a well-known best-selling novelist, and that had gotten him a reprieve from the mayor of Hampton Cove, but it didn't sit well with several concerned citizens that a cop on the Hampton Cove Police Department was an NYPD reject, so they'd been pressuring the council and Mayor Turner to have him dismissed.

Odelia had promised to look into the case, but so far had nothing to show for her efforts. If Chase's old boss was having an affair, he was very discreet about it, and so far she only had Chase's word on the matter.

As she was crossing the street to pick up the necessary ingredients for the chocolate cake her mother wanted her to bake, she saw a guy selling something from the trunk of his car, and she was reminded of Orville's words.

She decided to have a closer look and, arriving there, saw that the guy's customer was none other than her own grandmother! The feisty old lady was negotiating with the salesman, who stood gesticulating wildly. He had slicked-back raven hair and was wearing an actual three-piece suit.

"Gran?" she asked when she'd joined the odd couple. "What is this?"

"Oh, there you are, honey. I was hoping to run into you. So what do you think, huh?" she asked, holding up a small plastic baggie in one hand and a glass vial in the other. "Powder or liquid? I was thinking liquid, as you know I have trouble swallowing."

Odelia's eyes swiveled to the trunk of the guy's car, and when she saw the baggies of white powder, clear glass vials, more baggies with pills in different colors, she had a pretty good idea what was going on here. She directed a hard look at the guy. "Are you selling Liquid G to my grandmother?"

"Hey, she wanted something to help her sleep," the guy said, holding up his hands. He then tapped a small vial. "This will help her sleep just fine."

"This will help her sleep forever," Odelia said, planting her hands on her hips. "You're that drug dealer, aren't you? The one who's trying to muscle Orville Haggis out of the market?"

The guy took a good look at Odelia. "And you're that reporter, aren't you?"

"Odelia's the best reporter in town," said Gran proudly. "She's the one that catches all the bad guys before the cops ever do." She then grinned at the guy. "She even caught herself a drug dealer just before, didn't you, honey?"

Well, news certainly traveled fast. But then what else was new?

The next thing she knew, the guy slammed the trunk of his car closed, and then he was bolting away from them, barreling down the sidewalk.

"Oh, crap, not again," she groaned, and took off after the guy.

"You go get him, honey!" her grandmother yelled. "I'd help you catch him but my hip's acting up again! In fact now might be a good time to try this here happy stuff, just like the guy said." And she flicked the vial curiously.

Horrified, Odelia shouted over her shoulder, "Don't drink that, Gran!"

But even as she glanced back, she saw that the old lady was already knocking back the vial with visible relish. And as she was sprinting after her second drug dealer of the day, she managed to snatch her cell phone from her pocket and press it to her ear. "Chase? I'm on Main Street, chasing another drug dealer. And my gran just took a hit of GHB!"

# CHAPTER 12

*a* foot pursuit was even harder than a car chase, she discovered. The guy might be a little portly, but he was in great shape. In fact he was in much better shape than she was. She probably should have bought that elliptical trainer. She'd only run a couple hundred feet before a shooting pain attacked her spleen, or whatever organ was acting up. But thinking about how this asshole had sold GHB to her grandmother gave her the fuel to keep going.

"Hold it right there!" she yelled as the guy jumped over a Poodle on a leash and then veered right between two shops. "I just wanna talk to you!"

That wasn't necessarily true, of course. Well, she did want to talk to him, but she also wanted to slam his head against the pavement until he promised never to sell drugs to senior citizens again, or anyone else for that matter. Not that he would listen. Guys like that never listened. You had to lock them up.

She also hung a hard right and found herself hurtling down a narrow alley that opened up into a wider lane. She halted, hands on knees, panting heavily, and checked left and right. In every direction she was looking into the backyards of the houses on the next street, all neatly divided by hedges or fences. And the drug dealer, who clearly wasn't a customer of his own junk, was now vaulting over the fences like a regular steeplechaser!

She wiped the sweat from her brow and with a groan continued her pursuit. She wanted to say she was too old for this shit, but that wasn't true. She was simply not trained for this shit. And as she climbed the first fence, she hoped Gran hadn't taken an overdose of that horrible drug. If she had, she'd never forgive dealer guy. Instead of gracefully hopping over the fence like a member of SEAL Team Six, she dropped down into the yard, her jeans ripping when they caught on a rusty nail. And as she tumbled down, she crashed right into a barbecue set, which, luckily for her, wasn't switched on.

A couple, sitting on the deck, stared at her. "Is this for a contest?" asked the woman.

"I think it's for one of them reality shows," said her husband.

"It's neither," she said, scrambling to her feet. "I'm chasing a drug dealer."

"Oh. Right," said the woman, as if that made perfect sense.

"You go get him, honey," said the man.

"I will, if I survive," she said between two gasps.

She climbed the next fence, and thought that at this rate she would never get her man. But then, to her great surprise, she saw that she'd gotten her man already. He was lying sprawled on the lawn of the next family's garden, cursing loudly and nursing an injured shin as he rolled on his back. Apparently, when landing, he'd knocked his shin on the toy plastic castle that took up a big part of the garden. The two kids who'd been playing with the castle were staring at the man who'd suddenly interrupted their garden party, and then set off into the house, wailing loudly for their mommy.

Odelia pounced on the guy and pressed him face down into the grass. She would have loved to cuff him, but since she wasn't a cop she couldn't. She now wondered if it wouldn't be a good idea to ask Uncle Alec to deputize her, seeing as she was doing more work than the regular cops anyway.

But then her eye fell on a brightly green skipping rope, and she figured it would do. So she quickly and expertly tied the guy's hands.

"You have the right to remain silent," she began.

"What the hell are you doing?" he cursed, spitting out a few blades of grass. "You're not a cop! You can't make an arrest!"

"It's called a citizen's arrest, bozo," she said, and shoved his face into the grass again. "And shut up! You just tried to kill my grandmother!"

He lifted his face. "I didn't kill her!" he grunted. "I gave her a watered down vial of liquid G. She'll just be very happy for the next couple of hours."

"Still, you shouldn't sell that junk to people."

"Look, lady, I'm just trying to make a living here. So back off, all right?"

This lame excuse set her teeth on edge. "Is it true you were trying to muscle in on Orville Haggis's territory, yes or no?"

"Sure! That loser thinks he's the only one who can sell stuff in this town, and I'm here to show him he's wrong. You can't stifle competition! That's just plain wrong. What's more, it's un-American!"

"What's un-American is killing people. You killed John Paul George, didn't you? And then tried to pin it on Orville, getting rid of him altogether."

"What?! You're crazy! Why would I do that? Johnny signed

up with me. He said my stuff was better quality, and a lot cheaper, too. I made the deal last week. This time next month I was taking over as Johnny's official supplier of G. If I killed him I'd be killing the goose with the golden eggs! Especially since he said he was going to recommend me to all of his friends."

Just then, an elephant came crashing through the brush, but when Odelia looked up, she saw it wasn't an elephant but Chase Kingsley, and he looked as winded and red-faced as she was.

"Another one!" he cried when he caught sight of her. "You caught another drug dealer?!"

"Yup, I caught him for you and now he's all yours."

He threw up his hands in a gesture of exasperation. "What kind of town is this? This is worse than New York!"

After catching his breath, he hoisted this new guy up and outfitted him with a nice pair of gleaming handcuffs to replace the skipping rope. And as Chase led the guy away, through the house this time, past the astonished gazes of the couple who lived there, she told him what the dealer had told her.

"So Orville is in the picture again, huh?"

"Looks like. If this guy was taking over his clients, Orville might have taken it hard and decided to send Johnny a parting gift in the form of a poisoned vial. Take him out once and for all and pin the murder on this guy."

"Good work," Chase grunted. "Again."

"How is my grandmother?"

"I've never seen her happier. When I left she was singing the national anthem at the top of her voice, demanding that some store clerk hoist her up to the store roof and let her fly like Lady Gaga at the Super Bowl."

"See?" asked the dealer. "A little happy juice goes a long way!"

"You're going to look a lot less happy when I'm through with you," grunted Chase, giving the guy a shove.

And as they took the turn to the main road, they were getting a lot of attention, people up and down the street staring at the small procession of three: the drug dealer, the burly cop and the svelte blond reporter.

"You know, at this rate Uncle Alec is going to have to deputize me," Odelia said. "I've taken down more bad guys than all you cops combined."

"Don't even think about it," growled Chase. "You're not a cop and you should stop acting like one. You're just putting yourself in danger."

"I could be a cop. I obviously have mad skills."

"Uh-uh," he said, shaking his head. "It's bad enough I keep tripping over you everywhere I turn. I don't want you chasing people and arresting them."

"Still, it's definitely something to consider."

"Nah-ah. Never."

"You have to admit she'd make a great cop, though," the drug dealer said. "And a pretty one, too. We don't have a lot of pretty cops in this town."

"If I want your opinion, I'll ask for it," grunted Chase.

They'd arrived at the dealer's car, where now Chase's pickup stood, the police light flashing on the roof. Gran was seated inside the trunk of the car, her tush firmly planted amongst the drug paraphernalia the guy sold, and she had a happy grin on her face, her eyes a little misty. Mom was by her side, eyeing Odelia critically. "What did you give her? She's acting all weird."

"Me? I didn't give her anything!" cried Odelia. "She bought this stuff!"

"This is some good shit right here," Gran croaked, and cackled loudly.

"Oh, God," said Mom. "We better take her to see your father."

Five minutes later, Chase dropped the three of them off at the doctor's office, while he rode on to the police station to process the dealer.

"Don't forget about dinner, Chase!" Mom said before he rode off. "Odelia is baking a great chocolate cake, aren't you, Odelia?"

Yes, that was the most important thing right now: chocolate cake.

But Chase surprised her by yelling back, "I'm looking forward to it, Marge."

The day was turning out a little weird, she felt, what with the murder and drug dealer number one and drug dealer number two and now Gran's surprise love for GHB. She just hoped that the rest of the day would be less eventful, and that amongst the people Chase had arrested, at least one would turn out to be the killer. By the law of averages, that had to be so, right?

## CHAPTER 13

It had been a long day, and when Dooley and I couldn't find Odelia at the paper, or the library, or the doctor's office, we figured she must have gone home. Actually I was glad. I could use a nap. Us cats don't usually traipse around town all day. We're more the nocturnal kind, and for us daytime is naptime. But when duty calls, like now, we gladly sacrifice our beauty sleep for the more important stuff, like helping our human catch a killer. Though it's entirely possible Dooley and I were the exception to the rule in this.

When we arrived in our backyard, I saw to my elation that the glass sliding door was wide open, meaning Odelia was home. And if that hadn't given her away, the smell of freshly baked chocolate cake would have.

"Hey darlings," she said when she caught sight of us. She was seated at the kitchen counter, sipping from a cup of coffee. One look at the deep groove in her brow told me she hadn't had any luck catching the killer yet.

"Hey, honey," I said. "How's it going?

"Yeah, any luck cracking the John Paul George thing?" asked Dooley.

He'd hopped up onto a stool, and I followed his example, watching as Odelia stared at us a little sadly and shook her head. "No luck so far, fellas. I did arrest two drug dealers today, so here's hoping one of them did it. Though to be honest I doubt it. Drug dealers rarely kill their customers. At least not intentionally. And definitely not by putting spider venom in their product."

"Spider venom? Is that what killed Johnny?" asked Dooley.

"Looks like. A rare spider venom, too. Something called Australian funnel-web spider venom. Supposedly the deadliest spider in the world. Though whoever administered the poison didn't count on its effect being greatly diminished when ingested. The only reason the venom killed Johnny was because he had a weak heart."

I thought about this for a moment. She was right. Why would a drug dealer kill a client? It made no sense. He'd lose the client, ruin his reputation, and potentially lose his business. People don't respond well to traffickers dealing in death rather than bliss. "So what's your theory?" I asked.

"So far I've got no theory," she admitted, rising to check on her cake. "All I know is that we need to keep looking, because Uncle Alec thinks he's got his killer in Jasper, and I'm pretty sure the guy is totally innocent."

"I think so too," I admitted. Dooley and I quickly gave her the gist of the interviews with Johnny's seemingly endless row of boy toys, but there seemed to be little news in those testimonies for Odelia, and for once I felt a little helpless. There's only so much information a cat can glean from humans, and so far we hadn't found the one clue that would break this case wide open.

"I think you should keep investigating," I said. "If your

uncle thinks he's got his killer, he's going to stop looking, and send the wrong guy to prison."

"I know," said Odelia, and gave us both a rub on the head. "Thanks for being my perfect feline spies, you guys. How did you ever get so smart?"

"We're sleuthing cats," I said, swelling a little. "Sleuthing is in our blood."

"Yeah, Sherlock Holmes and Dr. Watson got nothing on us," said Dooley.

Odelia leaned on the desk and eyed us with a humorous glint in her eyes. "So who's Sherlock Holmes and who's Dr. Watson, I wonder."

"Why, I'm Sherlock, of course," said Dooley.

"How do you figure that?" I asked.

"I'm thin and handsome and you're fat and… well, not so handsome."

"I'm not fat!" I cried. "How many times do I have to tell you? I'm big-boned. Besides, Dr. Watson wasn't fat. He was buff and trim. And Sherlock Holmes wasn't handsome at all. He was… gaunt."

"Gaunt and handsome," Dooley insisted. "Just like me."

"I think you could both be Sherlock Holmes," said Odelia soothingly.

"Which would make Harriet Irene Adler," I said.

"Wasn't she Sherlock's girlfriend?" asked Odelia.

"She was Sherlock's femme fatale," I corrected her.

"She fell for Sherlock, just like Harriet fell for Brutus," said Dooley sadly.

"So actually Brutus is Sherlock," said Odelia teasingly.

"Brutus obviously is Professor Moriarty," I countered. "The evil genius who was Sherlock's greatest foe. Which makes me Sherlock."

"Fat chance," Dooley scoffed.

"Look, Brutus is my biggest foe," I said.

"Our biggest foe," he corrected. "And he stole Irene Adler from us."

"Brutus is going to solve this case," I told Odelia now. "And then he's going to tell Chase."

"Oh? And how does he think he's going to do that?" asked Odelia. "As far as I know Chase doesn't talk cat."

I shrugged. "He says he'll find a way."

Odelia smiled. "I'd like to see him try."

"Yeah, me too," said Dooley. "I don't think it'll work. And when he fails miserably, like he's bound to, Harriet will finally discover that the elephant in her room has feet of clay and isn't wearing any clothes."

"Um, I think you've got your metaphors mixed up, buddy," I said. "Either we're talking about the elephant in the room, or Brutus has feet of clay or the emperor has no clothes. You can't have all three."

"Why not? It's not like Brutus has any clothes. He's a cat. Cats don't wear clothes. And neither do elephants."

"Sure," I said, not wanting to get into another argument. Dooley was obviously feeling a little fragile right now. "You have to solve this murder before Brutus does," I told Odelia. "If he finds the killer he's going to get so cocky life with him will simply be unbearable. And Harriet will continue to put him on a pedestal, which means we'll have lost our best friend forever."

"Yeah, we've got to put that cat in his place by showing him how things are done around here," said Dooley. "We have to catch that killer."

But Odelia shook her head. "I'd like to help you, guys, but so far I have no clue. And I'm starting to think we haven't scratched the surface yet."

"The surface of what?" asked Dooley.

"Of the elephant," I muttered. Then, louder, I said, "Just follow the money. Isn't that how you solve a murder in the first place?"

"Care to explain yourself, Sherlock?" asked Odelia, amused.

"I mean, why do humans kill humans? It's not like with us cats, to eat them, right?"

"Not unless your name is Hannibal Lecter," she admitted.

"They kill for revenge, or love, or money," I quickly summed up. "And people like Johnny, who are loaded to the eyeballs, are obvious targets. So who stood to gain most from his death? Who's getting the Benjamins, baby?"

"Who's Benjamin?" asked Dooley, confused.

"It's a figure of speech," I told him. "I mean, who gets the money?"

Odelia gave me an appreciative look. "You know, you'd make a pretty good cop, Max. You, too, Dooley. And because you guys worked so hard today, I got you a special treat."

I exchanged an excited glance with Dooley. We were all for treats, especially after traipsing around town all day. So we both hopped down to the floor, and next thing we knew she'd set down a plate with two chicken wings and we found ourselves staring at them, a little disappointed.

"What's wrong?" she asked. "I thought you loved chicken wings?"

"Oh, we do," I assured her.

"It's just that…" Dooley began.

"We tasted some of Johnny's food this morning."

"And it was so good, you wouldn't believe."

"Yeah, just about the best stuff I've ever tasted."

Odelia frowned. "Don't keep me in suspense. What was it?"

"Pâté," we said in unison, and Odelia laughed.

"You guys," she said, "you know I can't afford that stuff on my measly salary. If you want to have pâté every day you're going to have to find yourselves another human. One who's as rich as John Paul George."

Dooley and I exchanged a glance again, and we both shrugged.

"Nah, that's all right," I said.

"Yeah, I think we'll stick around," said Dooley.

"Pâté is great," I explained.

"But a great human like you is better," Dooley finished the sentence.

She laughed again. "What a relief. I almost thought I'd have to look for other cats." She checked on her cake again and shook her head. "I can't believe I'm baking a cake for Chase Kingsley of all people."

"*Love is in the air,*" I sang.

"*Everywhere you look around,*" Dooley chimed in.

We'd been rehearsing the song during our nocturnal cat choir practice sessions, and it almost sounded like the original. Only a lot more howly.

"Yeah, yeah, don't rub it in," she grumbled.

She leaned against the counter, frown firmly in place again. "Follow the money, huh? Who gets to benefit the most from Johnny's death?"

"Johnny's family," I suggested.

"And Jasper," said Dooley.

"And Bryony Pistol," said Odelia.

"Huh? Who?" I asked.

"Johnny's wife. Apparently Johnny never divorced her."

"I didn't know Johnny had a wife," I said.

"Nobody did. Though I'm pretty sure by now my uncle does."

"We better ask Brutus what he knows," I said. "He's been glued to the police station all day. Maybe he picked up something we missed."

"Let's ask Harriet," Dooley suggested. "Brutus won't tell us a thing."

"Well, he's probably right. We wouldn't tell him anything either."

"You guys, why don't you kiss and make up with Brutus already?" asked Odelia. "Hasn't this feud between you gone on long enough?"

"Why don't you and Chase kiss and make up?" I threw back.

She blinked. "It's complicated," she admitted.

"Well, our relationship with Brutus is complicated too."

"Very complicated," Dooley said somberly.

"Why don't I talk to Chase about Brutus again?" Odelia suggested.

"That would be great," I said. "Just tell him to get rid of the brute. I'm sure there's plenty of room at the animal shelter."

"Or just donate him to charity," said Dooley, perking up slightly.

She laughed. "I doubt Chase will go for it. But I will talk to him."

Dooley put his head on his paws again. It was obvious that 'talking to Chase' wasn't going to cut it. The guy obviously held no sway over his cat.

Fifteen minutes later, the cake was ready, and Odelia took it out of the oven and walked it across the yard to her parents' yard. We followed her, even though we should probably have that nap now. But duty called.

Over at Marge and Tex's, everything was set for dinner, and Uncle Alec and Chase were already chatting up a storm with their hosts. They were all seated out on the deck, where dinner was going to be served. No sense in being cooped up inside when the weather was this nice. Two other guests that had arrived were Brutus and Harriet, who were lying on the porch swing Odelia's dad had installed a couple of weeks ago. They looked like two lovers in heat, and Dooley muttered, "Max, I can't do this. I'm going home."

"No, you're not," I said, stopping him with my paw. "The worst thing we can do right now is show Brutus that he's won. We need to stand firm, Dooley. We need to show he's just a guest, and we're masters of our home."

He sighed. "Why do I have the impression he's not buying any of that?"

"Because he's hard of hearing," I said. "All we need to do is yell harder."

I walked up to Brutus and Harriet, and jumped up to join them on the love seat. Dooley, meanwhile, decided to remain on the ground, staring up at the three of us gloomily.

"Hey, Brutus," I said, trying to sound like a master of my own home. "So have you cracked this case yet?"

"Not yet," he admitted with a smug smile. "But I'm getting there."

"That's great," I said. "So you're close to catching the killer, huh?"

"I'm almost ready to reveal his identity, yes," said Brutus.

Harriet, who'd been licking her fur—that kind of snowy white coat takes a lot of licks to keep looking so nice and shiny—sighed wistfully. "Brutus is so clever, Max. He's listened to all the interviews Chief Alec and Chase did today, and he's drawn a most fascinating conclusion. He's really nailed it."

"You did, huh?" I asked. "Well, to be honest I expected nothing less from you, Brutus. You are a policeman's cat, after all. A true detective."

"Glad you're finally seeing things my way, Maxie, baby," he sneered.

"Oh, but I certainly do," I assured him. "It's just that us

country bumpkins need more time to figure things out than you slick city cats."

"See?" he asked, addressing Harriet. "I told you those two morons would see the light. All right," he said now. "I don't see why I can't tell you. I know for a fact now that there wasn't just one killer. They were all in it together."

I raised my eyebrows. "Come again?"

"Don't you see?" he asked. "All those boy toys—"

"Or toy boys," Harriet supplied.

"Whatever. They're all in this together, see?"

I was reluctant to admit I didn't see, so I just goggled at him.

"They were all sick and tired of having to compete for the attention of the johnny up top, so they decided to do away with Johnny once and for all."

"I, um… I'm speechless," I admitted.

"Come on!" he said. "You see it all the time. Humans can only be humiliated by another human for so long, until they start fighting back. Just think of Caesar being killed by his senators. Or all those assassination attempts on Hitler's life."

"What have Caesar and Hitler have to do with John Paul George?"

"Everything! Johnny was lording over these guys. They were like his slaves, and slaves will always rise up against their oppressors. These boys were sick and tired of having to perform these… services, night after night. I mean, Johnny wasn't exactly Brad Pitt. The guy was fat and ugly, and not much fun to please. So they finally decided to whack the guy. They all got together and devised a plan and swore a sacred oath never to tell a soul."

"Like a conspiracy, huh?"

"Exactly! And since they all swore to keep the secret, there's no way Chase or the Chief are ever going to find out what happened." He grinned. "But I'm on to them. Listening to their testimonies convinced me they're hiding something. And I'm going to reveal their secret. Me! Brutus!"

"They might be hiding the fact that they're all working as escorts," I pointed out. "Which isn't something they want their families to know."

"No, they're all in this one big conspiracy to kill their oppressor," Brutus insisted, "and I'm going to reveal the truth to Chase very soon now."

Dooley, who'd been staring up at Brutus throughout this long harangue, now swallowed. "Cats rising up to kill their oppressor, huh? I like it."

"Not cats," Brutus corrected him lazily. "Boy toys."

"Or toy boys," said Harriet.

"Whatever. Boys deciding to stick it to the man. Make him pay for what he did to them. Finally end the era of oppression and humiliation."

There was a strange fire in Dooley's eyes, and I could see that Brutus's words had made a great impact on him. Suddenly I saw why. Killing Brutus, that slightly feverish look on Dooley's face said, that is what we should do.

I shot him a warning glance, but he simply waggled his eyebrows.

"So where did those boys get the poison?" I asked Brutus.

He waved a careless paw. "Those are minor details. I'm sure that you'll find that one of those guys had access to a stash of spider venom. Slipping some of it into Johnny's vial would have been a piece of cake."

"Maybe one of those boys is Australian," said Harriet.

"Good thinking, toots," said Brutus. He pointed at Harriet. "Smart as a whip, this one. Australian spider venom? The Australian boy toy did it."

"Or toy boy," said Harriet, putting her head on Brutus's shoulder.

"Yeah, yeah. Whatever."

Dooley, who'd been Harriet's number one admirer from the first, looked pained. To watch the cat you've loved for so long being reduced to playing second fiddle was definitely painful to watch, and even more for him.

Maybe there was something in Dooley's idea, as he now stared at me imploringly. I finally rolled my eyes and nodded. Maybe there was merit in this. If we couldn't get rid of Brutus the easy way, maybe we simply had to kill him. And that's how Operation Kill Brutus was born. Out of Dooley's love for Harriet, and my exasperation with the brute. Suddenly mixing some little-known exotic poison in the cat's food didn't sound all that far-fetched.

We might not have been Brutus's boy toys—or toy boys—but we were cats being oppressed by a brutal, well, oppressor, and ready to rise up. Now all we needed to do was find one of those Australian funnel-web spiders and convince him to loan us some of his venom. How hard could that be?

# CHAPTER 14

"So, Chase," said Odelia, once they were all seated at the dinner table. "When are you going to find yourself a place of your own?"

He gave her a level gaze. "Why, do you have a suggestion for me?"

"Chase will find a place when he's good and ready," said Mom. "In the meantime he's happy to stay with Alec, isn't that right, Alec?"

"Sure," said the Chief, ladling more mashed potatoes onto his plate and adding a good helping of gravy. "You're welcome to stay for as long as you like, Chase, I already told you that."

"Thanks, Chief," said Chase warmly, and popped a meatball into his mouth. "These meatballs are just great, Marge."

"Thanks," said Mom. "But it's actually my mother you should thank, Detective. She rolled them, isn't that right, Mom?"

Gran, who was still looking a little hyped up, nodded. "That's right. They're my specialty. Always had a keen interest in meatballs, if you catch my drift." At this, she

101

directed a look so lascivious at Chase, Odelia almost groaned in embarrassment. Dad had given her a quick checkup, and had said there was no danger. That the effects of the drug would wear off pretty soon. Apart from occasional hot flashes and a sense of euphoria, she'd be just fine. What he hadn't said was that she was going to be horny as heck. Which Odelia should probably have realized, cause that was exactly the reason John Paul George had been so fond of this particular substance.

"Yeah, you've got some amazing balls, Vesta," Dad said, oblivious.

"I know," said Gran, "and I'm not the only one." Once again, she shot some pretty lewd looks in Chase's direction. To his credit, the cop decided to steer the conversation to safer waters and away from the meatball theme.

"The reason I haven't found a place yet is because this town has some pretty expensive real estate," he said now.

"Yeah, you're right," said Dad. "Lots of folks have decided to profit from the boom by turning their houses into B & Bs and the rest have been snapped up by tourists. Hard to find something reasonably priced nowadays. Unless you're handy with tools? There's always a fixer-upper you can find, Chase."

"Oh, I'll bet he's real handy with his tools," said Gran, licking her lips.

"Well, I am," said Chase, after giving Gran a bemused look. "But not handy enough to fix up an entire house, I'm afraid."

"You'll find something," said Uncle Alec. "Until then *mi casa es su casa*."

"So have you made any progress on the JPG case yet?" asked Mom.

"Yeah, do you think you've got the right guy in custody?" asked Dad.

"Well, I'm still leaning toward Jasper," said Uncle Alec. "I really like him as a suspect. He had opportunity—he knew exactly which vial was Johnny's and he could easily have slipped in that venom—and he sure had motive, from what I can tell. And let's not forget that his fingerprints were all over that vial."

"Too bad," said Dad with a shake of his head. "I've gotten to like the guy. I would never have pegged him for a killer. Not in a million years."

"Sometimes it's the ones you least suspect," said the Chief.

"So what was his motive?" asked Dad. "Why did he do it?"

"The obvious one: money. He was slowly being edged out of Johnny's inner circle and that mustn't have sat well with him. It was only a matter of time before Johnny was going to ask him to pack his bags and clear out, and that would have been the end of his cushy life."

"But he's not going to inherit much, is he?" asked Odelia.

"He stands to inherit plenty," said Uncle Alec. "I talked to Johnny's lawyer and he said Jasper gets the house and a monthly allowance. That's plenty of motive right there. Plenty of folks would kill for a deal like that."

"But what about the bulk of the estate?" asked Odelia. "Who gets that?"

"Ah, now there's something interesting," said the Chief, wiping his lips on his napkin and placing it next to his plate.

"The wife," said Chase. "She gets the whole kit and caboodle."

Odelia noticed the detective didn't seem happy about it for some reason.

"We didn't even know there was a wife, did we, Chase?" asked the Chief.

"We sure didn't," he said, in the same subdued way.

"Not only was Johnny still married, Mrs. George inherits all."

"So what about Johnny's six sisters?" asked Odelia. She'd

read somewhere that Johnny had no less than six sisters, who lived in England.

"Whose sexy sisters?" asked Gran, confused.

"They'll get their share," the Chief confirmed, ignoring his mother, "but compared to what the wife gets that's just chump change."

"I knew about the wife," said Mom. "I didn't know she was still in the picture, though. She must be happy after the sacrifices she made."

"Sacrifices?" asked Chase.

"Yes, Mom told me that Bryony spent a fortune launching Johnny's career," said Odelia.

"Not just *a* fortune, her entire family's fortune," Mom corrected her.

"So I guess it's only fair she gets to recuperate it," Odelia said.

"So this wife," Dad said. "This… Bryony…"

"Pistol," Mom supplied.

"A real pistol," Gran murmured inexplicably, munching on a meatball.

"This Bryony Pistol," Dad continued. "Have you talked to her? Maybe she's got what you detectives call, um, means, motive and opportunity?" He smiled apologetically. "You can tell I'm not the sleuth in this family."

"We're going to interview her first thing tomorrow morning," said the Chief. He gave Chase a quick glance. "That is to say, I'm going to talk to her."

Odelia frowned at this. "Why not Chase?"

"There's a hitch," Chase said. "Turns out Bryony Pistol has a daughter—"

"Veronica George," the Chief said.

"—who filed a restraining order against me some time ago."

They all stared at him, stunned. "What do you mean?" asked Odelia.

Uncle Alec cleared his throat. "Talk about a small world, huh? Turns out Johnny's little girl, who's not so little anymore, used to date the scumbag you arrested today. Orville Haggis. Orville isn't his real name, though. He goes by the name Rubb. Donovan Rubb."

Gran, whose eyes had drooped closed, sat up with a start. "Rub? Rub who?"

The Chief stared at her for a moment, then continued, "Turns out Donovan Rubb and Veronica George are the ones that caused so much trouble for Chase. They're not an item anymore, but she's the one that filed those charges against Chase, and got him kicked off the force."

They all exchanged startled glances. "So you can't talk to her?" asked Mom. "That's just crazy."

Chase nodded. "I can't come within three hundred feet of the woman."

"Well, I'll be damned," said Dad, and his words spoke for all of them.

For a moment, a pregnant silence descended upon the company, until Gran croaked, "More meatballs anyone? Take 'em while they're hot."

"Why don't I go with you tomorrow, Uncle Alec?" Odelia suggested. "I mean, I have to talk to the widow anyway, for my article, so we might as well go together. Especially now that Chase can't come near the daughter."

"That's a great idea," said the Chief.

"That's a terrible idea," said Chase. "Come on, Chief. Odelia is not a cop. You can't bring her into this investigation."

"She's already front and center," said the Chief. "Or have you forgotten she's the one that nailed those two drug dealers? Besides, she's a great interviewer, that niece of mine. Aren't you, honey?"

"But this goes against every rule in the book," Chase protested.

"We're not big on rules down here," Gran piped up.

"Yeah, you'll find that we tend to do things different in Hampton Cove," said Dad, clapping the burly cop on the back. "And Odelia has a knack for solving mysteries."

"She used to try and solve mysteries when she was just a little girl," said Mom. "Tell Chase about that time you solved the teddy bear mystery, honey."

In spite of himself, Chase's lips quirked up into a grin. "Teddy bear mystery?"

"Not now, Mom," Odelia said, embarrassed.

"Odelia's favorite teddy bear went missing one day, and she wouldn't let it go," Mom said with a smile at the memory. "I just figured she'd lost it somewhere, you know, but she was adamant someone had kidnapped it."

"I remember that," said Dad, also smiling now.

"Turned out she was right. Billy Bob Turner, whose family used to live right across the street, had gotten it into his nut to collect all the bears from all the houses on the block and hide them under his bed. Turns out his folks were into some kind of religious cult and he thought the world was going to come to an end soon and he needed to save all the teddies of all the kids."

"Aw, that's actually kinda sweet," said Chase.

"So Odelia stomps over there one day and accuses Billy Bob of kidnapping her teddy and holding him hostage, and lo and behold, she was right. She'd found a small footprint right outside her window, and had tracked it all the way to the Turner place."

"Well, as much as I hate to tell you this, Marge, there's a difference between finding Mr. Teddy and catching a killer," said Chase. "This is some seriously dangerous stuff, and I don't think it's a good idea to involve untrained and unarmed civilians. And I'm only telling you this for her safety."

"Who says she's unarmed?" Gran now piped up.

"Gran, not now," Odelia hissed.

"Yes, Mom, not now," Chief Alec said, looking decidedly ill at ease.

"What do you mean, she's not unarmed?" asked Chase. "I checked the registry when I first arrived in town and your niece doesn't have a license."

"Of course she's got a gun," Gran insisted. "And she's a great shot, too."

"You checked my license?" asked Odelia, incensed.

"When I keep bumping into someone, I want to be sure they're not carrying," Chase said. "Call it my innate sense of self-preservation."

"You had no right," she began, but then realized he did have the right.

"Anyone want more meatballs?" Mom asked in a faux-chipper voice.

"She keeps it in her purse," said Gran now, "just like any girl should."

"So you're carrying a gun without a license. Why am I not surprised?"

"Chase," said Uncle Alec warningly.

"I can't believe you'd let your niece carry an illegal gun!"

"It's not her fault she lost her license!" Gran cried. "So back off, tightass."

"Lost her license? Why? Did she shoot somebody?" he asked. When she refused to look him in the eye, he cried, "You actually shot someone?!"

"He was a nobody," Gran supplied. "One of those no-good

107

boyfriends of hers. And good riddance, too. The guy was too old for her anyhoo."

Chase's eyebrows rose. "You killed him?!"

"Nah, she missed," said Gran.

"I didn't miss," she snapped. "If I wanted to kill him he'd be dead right now."

"Would have been better if you had," said Gran. "Piece of no-good scum."

"He was one of her boyfriends," Mom said when Odelia clamped her lips together. How had this conversation gotten away from her so fast?

"One of her no-good boyfriends," Gran said, rubbing it in.

"Odelia always had horrible taste in men," Mom said, quite unnecessarily.

"This one was even worse than the others, though," said Gran. "Talk about a loser."

Chase, shaking his head, asked, "Who was he? The bank robber? Or the crook wanted in six states?"

"Twelve states," Uncle Alec muttered. "But who's counting?"

Odelia looked up at Chase, and saw that a twinkle had appeared in his eyes. "If you have to know, he was a rookie cop," she finally said. "I was eighteen and he said that if I showed him mine he'd show me his. So I did, and accidentally shot his… package. Hey! He said he wanted to do it with the safety off!"

"Talk about unsafe sex," said Dad with an eyeroll.

## CHAPTER 15

That night, Dooley and I decided to go out to the house of John Paul George for a recital of the cat choir in honor of our now orphaned brethren and sisters. It was the right thing to do, we felt, as a treat to the cats who were now going to be pâté-less for the rest of their lives, and who, if Jasper was convicted of his boyfriend's murder, might never see each other again.

"It makes you think about your own mortality, doesn't it?" I asked as we trotted along in a slow procession to Johnny's expansive mansion.

"It sure does," said Dooley with a sigh.

Perhaps a dozen cats had decided to make the trek, which just went to show how popular JPG had been with Hampton Bay's cat population, and how legendary his pâté. Not that we would get any of that tonight. Or at least I didn't think so. Father Reilly's tabby Shanille was there, Stacy Brown's cat, and Kingman, of course, Wilbur Vickery's cat. Conspicuously absent were Brutus and Harriet, but then they hadn't been invited.

We'd started the choir purely for our own amusement,

and to give vent to the artistic talents of its members, but now, with this tragedy, we'd found a new purpose: to honor the cats of recently departed humans. In most cases they were taken in by relatives, though in rare cases they ended up at the animal shelter. Not that they were to be pitied. The Hampton Cove animal shelter was a well-funded operation, its animals well taken care of.

"I wonder what would happen to us if anything ever happened to Odelia or her mom," said Dooley now, striking the morbid note.

"I'm sure nothing will happen to Odelia," I told him. "She's perfectly healthy and perfectly capable of taking care of herself. And us."

"Yeah, but it's still a possibility, isn't it?"

"I suppose so," I admitted. I didn't want to dwell on such a ghoulish and depressing topic, even though we were about to organize what was essentially a wake. "I think Odelia will have a long and prosperous life."

Dooley heaved a deep sigh. "I sure hope so."

We finally arrived at Johnny's mansion and gathered in a circle outside the wrought-iron gate where fans and towns-folk had placed dozens, perhaps even hundreds of floral tributes. They were piled up high against the fence, accompanied by candles and cards and all manner of commemorative gifts people had left behind. The outpouring of grief and love was impressive, and reminded us how beloved the singer had really been, and not just by cats.

We stepped through the gate's bars, and proceeded to the house, walked around back until we reached the pool area, and took a moment to gaze at the place where the great man had breathed his final breath. George, Princess and the other cats were all seated on pool chairs, and joined us in this silent tribute. Father Reilly's Shanille then spoke a few words in honor of the singer while we all stood there, heads bowed, listening to the brief sermon, which centered on the topics of ephemerality and the importance of enjoying every moment life so graciously gave, for you never knew what the future held.

And then we all broke into song, choosing for this opportunity a song of John Paul George himself, the rather apt 'Queen in a King-Size Bed,' one of his biggest hits. We massacred the popular hymn with glee, Kingman leading the choir and the rest of us meowing, yowling and caterwauling up a storm. Johnny's twelve cats, after listening with rapt attention for a while, soon joined in, and for the next twenty minutes or so, nothing could be heard but the sweet sound of two dozen cats screeching at the top of their lungs.

I don't know if the neighbors could hear our very special midnight concert and frankly I didn't care. But if they had, I'm sure they would have appreciated it as much as I did. At one point a window was thrown open upstairs and a curler-covered woman's head appeared, shouting something and throwing a shoe. It made a nice splash as it landed in the pool, and the head disappeared again, grumbling some choice curse words under its breath.

All in all, the tribute went well, and I was truly moved, and even had to wipe away a tear, as did most of the other cats. A few of them were even wailing and crying their eyes out, and even George, probably the oldest cat in our small feline gathering, was sniffling softly into his whiskers.

When the concert was over, Johnny's cats thanked us, and then led us all inside to sample some of Johnny's special pâté. It was a testament to the special moment that they all shared their bowls with us, and I was happy to see they were filled to the brim, which told me that even in Johnny's and Jasper's absence, their feline friends were well looked after. Possibly by the woman in curlers who'd just thrown her shoe at us.

After everyone had eaten their fill, we walked out again,

and we all sat around carefully licking our paws and cleaning our faces. Dooley and I took this opportunity to chat with Princess. The Siamese was more subdued than before, which wasn't hard to understand.

"That was very sweet of you," she said with a little sniffle.

"Just showing our appreciation for what Johnny meant to the world," I said.

"I'm sure he would have loved it. Too bad he isn't here to enjoy it." She glanced up at the sky. "Or maybe he is."

Dooley and I also looked up at the twinkling stars. "Yeah," I said with a smile. "I'm sure he's up there looking down at us right now."

Just at that moment, a star sparkled, and Princess gasped, clutching at her heart. "I'm sure that was Johnny, letting us know how much he cares."

We stared up for a while longer, but I decided to strike the business note again. We weren't just here for the tribute and the pâté, after all, but also to solve a murder. "Our human is having a chat with Johnny's wife tomorrow."

"Oh, that's nice," she said vaguely, not showing the least bit of interest.

"Did you know he was still married?" I tried again.

She nodded. "Mh-mh. Though the last couple of years she rarely came out here. She wasn't very fond of Jasper, as you can imagine."

"She wasn't, huh?" I asked, with a meaningful glance at Dooley, who was staring at Princess now, who was still staring up at the stars.

"He was writing again, you know," she said dreamily.

"Writing? You mean songs?"

"No, the great American novel," she said. "Of course songs, silly. I told you last time that he had hundreds of songs tucked away, but lately he'd been having trouble focusing and he'd stopped recording altogether for the past year or so. Until he decided to get into the groove again. He wanted to keep it a secret from Jasper, though. A special surprise for their anniversary. They would have been together fifteen years next month, and he wanted to surprise him by presenting him with an entire album of brand new songs."

"I thought he'd stopped recording altogether. That he had trouble with his voice. At least that's what Jasper told the police."

"Well, he had, but he was working with a voice coach, and things were progressing nicely. His voice had a different timbre," she said softly. "More mature, but still very much Johnny. And his songs were different, too. More reflective, and completely acoustic. Just Johnny and his guitar." She sighed wistfully. "I thought they were some of his very best work. Pity the world will never get to hear them."

"Why not?" I asked. "If Jasper finds those recordings he might release them as a treat to Johnny's fans."

"I doubt it," she said sadly. "With Jasper in prison, the care of Johnny's estate will probably fall on his wife now, and since Jasper is the only one with access to Johnny's computers, she won't even know about the music."

"Unless we tell Jasper and he tells the wife," I said.

She eyed me strangely. "How can you tell Jasper? You don't speak human."

"No, I don't, but my human speaks cat, so there's that."

She smiled, obviously not believing a word I'd just said.

"It's true," Dooley chimed in. "We can talk to our human."

"Sure," she said. "Whatever you say, guys."

"Princess?" George asked from the house. "Are you coming?"

"Yes, George," she said, then turned to us. "Time for my beauty sleep. Thanks for the tribute concert. It was wonderful."

"Thanks for the pâté," said Dooley with a dumb grin on his face.

She smiled. "You're welcome."

We watched as she sashayed in the direction of the house.

"Wow," said Dooley finally. "What a cat."

"Yeah," I managed, though a little huskily. "What a cat."

# CHAPTER 16

$\mathcal{O}$delia had a hard time finding sleep. Long after she should have drifted off into a refreshing slumber, she was still tossing and turning. She couldn't stop thinking about the murder case, and how her uncle was sure he got the right man in jail. Even though he'd agreed to interview the widow, he considered it a mere courtesy call. She was convinced that Jasper was innocent, and not just because her father thought so, too. There was something fundamentally wrong about this whole case.

For one thing, the fingerprints on the vial were too convenient. If Jasper had gone to all the trouble of collecting the venom of a rare species of spider, would he really be so dumb to leave his fingerprints behind? She didn't think so. Those prints had to have been planted there. And where had Jasper found that venom? It wasn't as if they sold that stuff at Walmart or Target.

The chief assumed he'd gotten it online, or from a friend, but so far he had to admit they hadn't tracked down either this friend or the site where Jasper could have bought it, and Odelia was pretty sure he never would.

When finally she'd drifted off into a restless sleep, she was awakened by the familiar weight of Max finding his space at the foot of the bed. She smiled. He'd been off half the night, as usual, and she was glad he was back.

"How was your evening, Max?" she whispered, raising her head from the pillow to look at the familiar form of the big, ginger cat. He stared back at her with his remarkable cat's eyes, lit up by a sliver of moon slanting in through the curtains.

"We did a memorial concert for Johnny," he whispered back. "His cats were all deeply touched."

"Why are you whispering?" she whispered.

"Because you are whispering!"

"Oh. Right. Well, that was very sweet of you."

"Did you know that Johnny was recording again?"

"He was? I thought Jasper said he'd lost his voice?"

"Well, he had, but he was practicing with a voice coach and was writing new songs. He'd recorded a bunch of acoustic songs for Jasper, as a surprise for their fifteenth anniversary. He was going to give it to him next week."

She thought about this. If Johnny was recording songs for Jasper, he wasn't going to leave him, was he? And that put that particular motive to rest once and for all.

"You have to tell Jasper," said Max. "Otherwise those songs will be lost forever. They're on Johnny's computer, and Princess said only Jasper has the password."

"Princess?"

Max hesitated. "One of Johnny's cats. A Siamese."

She smiled in the darkness. "Is she nice, this Princess?"

"She's all right," he said. "Dooley ate all of her food the other morning, but since she didn't say anything about it, I guess she didn't even notice."

"People like Johnny have housekeepers, Max, and lots and

lots of staff. I'm sure they don't personally deal with minor details like feeding the cats."

"That's what I told Dooley!" He paused, then said, "I'm glad you take care of these minor details, Odelia." His voice suddenly sounded husky.

"I like taking care of those details."

There was a pause, then Max said, "Thanks."

"You're welcome, honey."

She'd almost drifted off to sleep when he asked, in a small voice, "Odelia?"

"Mh?"

"What's going to happen to me if something happens to you?"

"Nothing's going to happen to me, Max. I promise."

"That's what I told Dooley," he said, and he seemed satisfied, for a few minutes later she heard his typical light snore softly echoing through the room. The sound soothed her, and before long she was fast asleep herself.

# CHAPTER 17

The next morning saw Odelia, bright and early, swing by the police station to see her uncle. When she breezed into the Chief's office, not bothering to knock as usual, she found both her uncle and Chase looking downcast, as if they had something on their minds.

She dropped down into the seat next to Chase. "Why the long faces, guys? Bit in a bad donut?"

"If only that were true," grunted her uncle.

She glanced over at Chase, but he refused to meet her gaze.

"So? Don't keep me in suspense. What's wrong?"

Uncle Alec leaned back, his chair creaking beneath his bulk. "We've been overruled by the powers that be, I'm afraid."

She gave him a blank stare. "I have no idea what you just said. What powers that be? What did they overrule?"

"I just got a call from the mayor, demanding we release Donovan Rubb, aka Orville Haggis, at once."

She sat bolt upright at this. "Release Donovan Rubb? But why?"

"Turns out the mayor got a call from Chase's old boss, NYPD Commissioner Vernon Necker, conveying his displeasure with Mr. Rubb's arrest. When he heard Chase was involved, he pretty much blew a gasket."

"But he can't force you to release Rubb, can he? That's just nuts."

"Well, technically the mayor can't interfere in an ongoing investigation, but if he wanted to he could have my job, so…"

She stared at her uncle. "Fire you? You've got to be kidding me."

"He didn't actually tell me he was going to fire me, but it was implied."

"Is this still about that same nonsense with the Commissioner?"

"It is," Chase confirmed.

Her uncle sighed deeply. "Rubb must have asked his lawyer to put in a good word for him with his old buddy Commissioner Necker—"

"Who decided to intervene in an ongoing murder investigation?"

"Looks like."

"But you refused, right?" she asked. When her uncle didn't respond, she repeated, a little more heatedly, "Tell me you refused, Uncle Alec."

"Donovan Rubb walked half an hour ago," said Chase.

"Are you crazy?! The man's a drug dealer! You can't let him walk."

"Afraid I had no choice in the matter," said the Chief. "Rubb claims police harassment."

"He confessed! He told us he sold those drugs to John Paul George!"

"He retracted that statement. Said it was given under duress. Says you roughed him up and he's got the scrapes and bruises to prove it."

"He rode his bike into a ditch, which is how he got the scrapes and bruises."

"He says you put him in that ditch. By forcing him off the road. He's pressing charges for police brutality and he's got the Commissioner in his corner."

"Well, I'm not a cop, so he can't sue me for police brutality."

"He's still pressing charges, against both you and Chase." He shook his head. "And that's not even the worst part."

"It gets worse?"

"When the Commissioner heard about Chase's involvement he wasn't pleased. So he gave the mayor to understand he was doing Hampton Cove a disservice by having a man of his reputation carry a badge in this town."

She looked from her uncle to Chase. "He's trying to get you fired?"

"Well, obviously the mayor can't fire Chase, only I have that authority," said Uncle Alec, "but he made it clear that he wasn't happy with my decision to hire Chase in the first place, and he wants Chase gone. Right now."

She sagged a little. This was terrible. She and Chase didn't always see eye to eye—well, actually they never saw eye to eye on anything, and had locked horns several times. But he was a good cop and these charges were bogus.

"So what are you going to do?" she asked.

"In all good conscience I can't fire Chase," said the Chief. "I just can't."

"Which is why I've decided to step aside myself," said Chase.

"You're leaving?" she asked.

"Yes, I am. I think it's extremely noble of you to try and protect me, Chief, but I can't put you in this position. It's not fair to you or the people of this town. If the mayor wants me gone, I'm going." He shook his head. "No sense postponing the inevitable and dragging this out. We all knew this was coming sooner or later, and arresting that scumbag Rubb seems to have sped up the process."

"But you can't go," she said. "You did nothing wrong."

He fixed her with a curious look. "You believe that?"

"Of course I do. This whole thing is a setup. All you need to do is clear your name. If you can prove you were set up, this will all go away."

"That's a pretty big if."

"Not if you've got Hampton Cove's number one reporter on your side."

He grimaced. "Look, this is not the first time I've gone through this. I'd hoped I could leave it all behind, but obviously that's not the case, so…"

"You can't give up now, Chase. This is just wrong."

"This is politics."

She frowned. "What if you talked to the mayor of New York? I'm sure he'll believe you if you tell him his wife is having an affair. He'll be furious."

"The mayor of New York knows perfectly well his wife is having an affair, and he doesn't give a hoot. Probably because he's having an affair himself."

"With the Commissioner's wife? That would be funny."

He looked at her from beneath lowered brows. "I'm not laughing."

"If the mayor knows, why isn't he divorcing her?"

"I told you, he doesn't care. All he cares about is that his wife is funding his reelection campaign, so he's not going to rock the boat. Or cause a scandal. They're presenting a united front, all to further his political ambitions. So when some pesky cop comes along, they simply crush him."

Things were becoming a lot clearer now. Inadvertently

Chase had stuck his head into a hornet's nest, and whatever he did, he wasn't getting out without being stung. "So what are you going to do? Lay down and die?"

He smiled a thin-lipped smile. "I'm going to save your uncle the trouble of having to deal with my mess." He placed his badge and his gun on the Chief's desk and rose. "Thanks for the opportunity, Chief. It's been a real honor."

"But you can't go," she said. "This town needs a cop like you, Chase."

She couldn't believe she'd just said those words, and meant them, too.

"Thanks for allowing me to see you in action, Miss Poole. It's been a real treat, and I'm not likely to forget those remarkable driving skills of yours."

And then, before she could say something else, he simply walked out.

She sat there, staring at her uncle, who looked just as shocked as she did.

"This isn't right," she told him. "In fact this is all kinds of wrong."

"Tell me about it," he grumbled. "This is a hit job."

"I'm going to clear Chase's name," she said decidedly.

"And how exactly are you going to do that?"

"I have no idea," she said. She saw that Brutus and Harriet were seated on the windowsill, listening attentively. They looked equally stunned.

"You know you surprise me," said her uncle. "I actually thought you'd be glad to be rid of Chase. Hell, I figured you'd be jumping for joy right now."

"I'm not saying that Chase doesn't have his faults," she said. "But he's a good cop, and this town needs men like him. Granted, the way he always wants to do things by the book is infuriating, but I'd hate to see him go."

"He is a great cop," said the chief. "And I hate to see him go, too."

"I'm going to fix this mess," she said. "I don't know how, but I will."

# CHAPTER 18

*B*efore Odelia could devote her attention to getting Chase's name cleared, she had a murder to solve, though. So half an hour later, she and her uncle were seated across from Bryony Pistol, John Paul George's widow. She was the same age as the singer, but looked at least a decade younger, so either she had killer genes, or had taken a leaf from Jennifer Aniston's page and copied the actress's anti-aging secrets.

"Thanks for seeing us on such short notice, Mrs. George," the Chief said.

"Pistol. I rarely use my husband's name these days."

"Mrs. Pistol. And my condolences for your loss."

"Thank you, Chief," said the woman, dabbing a small handkerchief to her eyes. She was sitting ramrod straight, the picture of regal grace and poise.

The house where she lived wasn't as big or luxurious as Johnny's, but it was still very nice, and it was obvious that the woman was well-off.

"I'd actually hoped to talk to your daughter, too," said the Chief.

"Yes, I'm sorry about that. Veronica had an urgent meeting in town. She should be back soon." She eyed Odelia a little uncertainly. "Are you also a police officer, dear?"

"Miss Poole is a, um, consultant," said the Chief. "She's also my niece."

"What about that other policeman? What's his name, um…"

"Detective Kingsley is no longer on the case, ma'am. In fact he doesn't work for us anymore as of this morning."

Bryony nodded. "My daughter will be pleased to hear that."

"About your daughter… is it true she used to be involved with Donovan Rubb?"

"I'm sorry to say that she was, even though I always told her not to be. Perhaps you already know this, but Mr. Rubb used to deal drugs, you see."

"We know," the Chief confirmed. "He was Johnny's supplier."

"Oh, dear," said the woman, shaking her head in obvious dismay. "Good thing Veronica broke up with him. That man would have been her downfall."

"When exactly did they break up, ma'am?"

"Well, let me see." She thought for a moment. "I'm pretty sure it was soon after that incident with Detective Kingsley. She finally came to her senses."

"Sorry to interrupt," Odelia said. "But what exactly happened between Detective Kingsley and your daughter?"

The woman raised her hands and dropped them in her lap. "Well, he made a pass at her, didn't he? He interviewed her when Donovan got arrested and must have taken a fancy to her, because he tried to kiss her."

Chief Alec cleared his throat and gave his niece a warning look. "After your daughter and Mr. Rubb broke up, did they keep in touch?"

"Not to my knowledge. I actually took this house after this whole affair ended, just to make sure Veronica would be away from her old circle. Away from the temptations of the big city and that toxic group of so-called friends of hers." She waved a hand. "And also to be closer to her father, of course, though God knows Johnny was never much of a father to Veronica, or a husband to me, for that matter. Still, it was better than staying in New York."

"You do know that Mr. Rubb also moved out here, don't you?" asked Odelia. "He was operating a health food store under an assumed name."

"Orville Haggis," the Chief muttered.

"No, I did not know that," said Bryony. "But I'm not surprised. That man always had an unhealthy obsession with my daughter. At least she was over him. Said she'd learned her lesson. Besides, she could see what drugs were doing to her father, and I like to think that's the wake-up call she needed."

"Did you and Johnny remain close?" asked Odelia.

"Yes, we did. In fact we never even bothered to get divorced. Though these past few months we'd discussed it. Johnny had big plans, you see."

Odelia frowned. "What plans?"

"Well, he was going to divorce me and marry Jasper, of course."

"You were going to divorce?" asked Odelia, surprised.

She nodded. "Johnny and I never went through the hassle of a divorce because we went from being lovers to being husband and wife to being best friends. I never blamed him for leaving me, and he always remained grateful for the support I gave to him in the early stages of his career." She smiled. "But when Johnny confessed he'd found a soulmate in Jasper and wanted to place their relationship on a more formal footing, I naturally agreed. We'd gone to see a lawyer together and were going to finalize the divorce so Johnny could have the big, fancy wedding he dreamed of."

"Who knew about this?" asked the Chief, as surprised as Odelia.

"Why, only Johnny and myself, of course. And the lawyer."

"Did Jasper know?" asked Odelia.

Bryony smiled. "Johnny wanted to keep it a secret. He was going to surprise Jasper with a romantic wedding proposal on their anniversary. Johnny had even recorded an entire album, as a wedding present."

"So you knew about the recordings?" asked Odelia.

"Of course." She sighed. "I'm sure they'll be posthumously released now."

"But what about all the… the escorts?" asked the Chief.

She made a throwaway gesture. "Oh, that. That was nothing, Chief. Johnny was a vigorous and very physical man who had certain needs, but those boys didn't mean anything to him. That was just sex, nothing more."

"But didn't Jasper find it strange that the man who told him he loved him was… inviting all these other men into his bedroom to, um, do stuff?"

"Do stuff? Oh, you mean sex. You could ask me the same thing. He started this habit when we were still married. Jasper wasn't the first."

"And did you? Mind, I mean?" asked Odelia.

The woman thought for a moment. "It didn't take me long to figure out that Johnny was a very complicated man, and that he was never going to be fully mine. Like the cliché goes, a star belongs to the whole world, and Johnny took that quite literally. I can't deny that when I first became aware of his infidelities I was disappointed, even heartbroken, but he promised me it didn't lessen how he felt about me, and I believed him. Johnny compared his nocturnal acrobatics to going to the gym. For him those boys were simply exercise, and he never formed an emotional attachment to them. Until…"

"Until Jasper," Odelia supplied softly.

She nodded, and smiled a little wistfully. "Until Jasper. I lost Johnny, then. Before, he was simply experimenting, but with Jasper it was decided that I wasn't going to be his life partner after all. It stung, I won't deny that."

"But why did he keep having these fleeting affairs?" asked the Chief.

"Like I said, Johnny was a star, Chief. I don't expect you to understand. Being in a relationship with a genuine rock star is a very unsettling experience, while at the same time very exciting." She paused. "I'll miss him."

"Do you have any idea who might have done this?" asked Odelia.

She shook her head. "I have absolutely no idea, Miss Poole. He was a very sweet man, and as far as I know he had no enemies. All I can think is that one of the boys he slept with had hoped to replace Jasper, and when he saw he didn't stand a chance, took revenge in the worst possible way."

The chief nodded. "My theory is that Jasper is the one who killed your husband, Mrs. Pistol. He didn't like Johnny's, um, appetite and snapped."

"Oh, no," said the woman adamantly. "Like I said, Johnny planned to marry Jasper. So there was absolutely no reason for Jasper to kill him."

"But Jasper didn't know that," said the Chief. "You said so yourself."

"Jasper didn't know what?" suddenly a voice sounded behind them.

# CHAPTER 19

"Oh, darling, there you are," said Bryony. A dark-haired young woman had walked in and took a seat on the arm of her mother's Chesterfield. "These people are from the police. I was just telling them that Jasper didn't know Johnny wanted to marry him."

"You knew about this?" asked the Chief.

"Of course she did," said Bryony. "I have no secrets from my little girl."

"I'm sorry I couldn't be here sooner," said Veronica. "I had a small errand to run in town. I came back as soon as I could."

"Just a few quick questions if you don't mind, Miss George," said the Chief.

"Of course," she said as she gave her mother a kiss on the top of her head.

Outside, the birds were chirping, and Odelia could see through the open French windows that Bryony's garden was a regular floral delight. The woman noticed she was looking and said, "I just love flowers, don't you, Miss Poole?"

"I do," she admitted, "though I'm afraid I don't have a

green thumb like you obviously have. You have a beautiful home and a beautiful garden, Mrs. Pistol. I envy you."

"Thanks. That's why I prefer living in the country. Out here I can have a garden, while back in Manhattan I had to make do with my small balcony."

"Oh, Mother, you had more than just a small balcony. You had an entire greenhouse on the roof. And possibly the biggest one in the whole city."

"Yes, but that's hardly the same as a garden, darling."

"It was nice enough. To sit there on the roof, surrounded by all that floral splendor, while the city hummed on beneath us. It was simply heaven."

"It was, wasn't it?" asked Bryony.

The Chief cleared his throat at this point. All this talk about flowers and gardens clearly didn't hold his interest. "Miss George, do you have any idea who might have wished your father harm?"

"I don't," she said. "My father was the kindest, sweetest man in the world. He might have had his vices, but he would never hurt a fly and was kind to anyone he met. I honestly can't imagine anyone wanting to hurt him."

"What about… your ex-boyfriend? Donovan Rubb?"

A cloud passed over the woman's face. "Donny is a mistake from my past, Chief, as I'm sure my mother told you. I haven't seen him in a long time, and I hope to keep it that way. That said, I don't think he's capable of murder."

"Did you know he was your father's supplier of GHB?" asked Odelia.

"And that he supplied the fatal vial? The one that killed your father?"

"I didn't know that," she admitted. "But Donny would never kill anyone. He might be a weak man, and a criminal," she quickly added when her mother gave her a stern look, "but he's not a murderer. No way."

"You never bumped into him when you went to visit your father?" asked the Chief.

"Never." She stared down at her mother. "Do you think Daddy knew about Donny and only invited me over when he wasn't there?"

"That would have been so typical of him," said Bryony.

"Always trying to protect the ones he loved," said Veronica, and bit her lip as her eyes grew moist. "He really was the most wonderful father."

If Johnny cared so much about his daughter's well-being, why didn't he get a different drug dealer? Odelia thought. Maybe he only found out about Donovan Rubb after his daughter and ex-wife moved into town, and that's why he tried to change dealers? It definitely was something to look into. Somehow she had a feeling that Rubb made for a much better suspect than Jasper. Though how the latter's fingerprints had ended up on the vial was still a mystery.

"They fired that horrible Detective Kingsley this morning, darling," said Bryony now. "Isn't that the most wonderful news?"

The Chief shuffled his feet uncomfortably, and Odelia felt a rush of blood to her face. Even though she'd told herself not to bring up the business of the young woman's lies, it was hard not to do so after this.

"That's great, Mother," said the young woman distractedly.

"I told the Chief how Detective Kingsley tried to kiss you," Bryony went on. "And how you had no choice but to press charges against him."

"Speaking of Detective Kingsley," said Odelia, ignoring her uncle's warning look. "What is your comment on the persistent rumors, Miss George?"

"What rumors?"

"The rumors that you and Donovan Rubb made some

kind of deal with the NYPD. In exchange for the department dropping all charges against Mr. Rubb, you were asked to testify against Detective Kingsley."

A flush had crept up the young woman's face. "Who says so?"

"Well, word on the street is that Detective Kingsley saw something he wasn't supposed to see and to make him go away trumped-up charges were fabricated and his reputation destroyed. Would you like to comment?"

"Oh, God," groaned the Chief.

"Would I like to comment?" asked Veronica. "What kind of a police officer are you?"

"She's not a police officer, darling," said her mother. "She's a consultant and Chief Alec's niece."

"A consultant? You sound like a reporter," snapped Veronica.

"That's because I am a reporter," said Odelia.

The young woman's eyes narrowed. "I see. And you're present at a police interview, why, exactly?"

"That's none of your business," said Odelia, now also heating up.

"Well, my business with Detective Kingsley is none of yours, Miss Poole." She frowned. "Poole... Odelia Poole? The reporter for the Hampton Cove Gazette?"

"One and the same," Odelia said brightly.

The woman's teeth came together with a click. "I'm not saying another word. This is an outrage!"

"Just the way they do things in these small towns, darling," said her mother, darting nervous glances at the Chief, whom she obviously held in high regard.

"Well, I'll have to have a word with the mayor about this," said Veronica.

"Just like you had a word with the Commissioner about 'Donny's' arrest?" asked Odelia.

Veronica lifted her chin. "I have no idea what you're talking about."

"Someone told Commissioner Necker that Donovan Rubb had been arrested. He talked to Mayor Turner and the mayor leaned on my uncle to have Rubb released from prison and Detective Kingsley fired."

"I don't know where you get your information, Miss Poole—though I have my suspicions," she added with a pointed look at Uncle Alec, "but I can assure you I had nothing to do with that. I imagine that if anyone told the Commissioner about Donny's arrest it was Donny himself or his lawyer. Like I said, I haven't been in touch with him since we broke up, and I filed a restraining order against him for good measure."

"You do like your restraining orders, don't you, Miss George?"

"That's it," she snapped, getting up. "I want you out of here right now!"

"Veronica, darling," said her mother. "They're the police."

"He is, but she most certainly isn't. You can stay," she told the Chief. Then she turned to Odelia. "But I'm not saying another word as long as you are here."

Damn, Odelia thought. Now she'd gone and done it. She just had to go and flap her gums about Chase, hadn't she? Instead of playing it cool, she had to antagonize this woman and put all her cards on the table. But then she couldn't stand injustice, and the lies this woman had told about Chase simply rubbed her the wrong way. If she'd lied about Chase, what else was she lying about? Her relationship with Rubb? Was she still secretly in touch with him?

"I think you better wait outside, Odelia, honey," said the Chief now.

"Yes, please get out of my house, Miss Poole," Veronica said, hands on her hips now, eyes blazing.

And as Odelia left the room, she heard Bryony say, "It is highly unorthodox to have a reporter present at a police interview, isn't it, Chief?"

Yes, it was highly unorthodox, and if it was true that Veronica was still secretly seeing Rubb, she just might talk to the Commissioner again, who might talk to Mayor Turner, who might talk to Dan and force him to fire her, just like they'd leaned on her uncle to fire Chase.

Darn it. She'd just landed herself in a big ol' heap of trouble, hadn't she?

# CHAPTER 20

Seated in her uncle's squad car, she was waiting nervously until he came out. After what seemed like forever, he finally appeared on the doorstep and, after shaking hands with Bryony, ambled over and heaved his bulk into the driver's seat.

"Well?" she asked

"Well, that was some show, honey."

She groaned. "I know. I got carried away. But when I think of all the lies Veronica told I couldn't just sit there and say nothing. God knows she's put Chase through hell, and I'm sure she's not telling the truth about Rubb. I'm pretty sure she's still seeing that guy."

He turned to her with a serious expression on his face. "Odelia, honey, she's going to talk to the mayor, who apparently is a friend of the family."

She felt her blood run cold. "So? I'm not a cop. He can't do anything."

"Knowing Mayor Turner, and how much he likes his celebrities, he'll want to have a word with Dan. And me," he said, turning his gaze to the windshield. "About allowing you to tag along on official police business."

"You mean you might get into trouble because of me? I'm so sorry, uncle."

"That's all right. Mayor Turner isn't my first mayor. I've had worse. But he might raise Cain with that editor of yours. Though knowing Dan he'll probably flip the mayor the bird and tell him to take a hike."

She smiled. "He probably will." Still, she felt bad about having caused both her uncle and Dan so much trouble.

"Anyhoo," said her uncle, firing up the engine, "looks like I can put this case to rest now."

"What do you mean?"

"I mean I've got my suspect, and I've interviewed pretty much everyone connected to this case. So now it's up to the prosecutor to get a conviction."

Alarmed, she turned to him. "You're not going to charge Jasper?"

"Of course I'm charging Jasper. He's got motive, means and opportunity. The perfect trifecta. Of all the suspects, we're most likely to convict him."

"But he didn't do it. Even Bryony said he would never harm Johnny."

"He was a boy toy past his prime, honey. He saw other, younger guys moving in and he knew it was only a matter of time before he was out."

"But Johnny was going to marry him!"

"He didn't know that. If he had, things might have gone differently."

She shook her head. "I'm sure he didn't do it."

"You keep forgetting his fingerprints were on that vial, Odelia. This is an open-and-shut case from where I'm sitting, and I'm sure the District Attorney's Office will agree with me on that. Easiest conviction ever."

"This isn't over yet," she grumbled, putting her feet up on the dash.

He grimaced. "Are you sure you aren't part bloodhound, honey?"

She very well might be. Her uncle dropped her off at the newspaper, and she went in to find Dan and tell him to expect a call from the mayor.

"Let him call," said Dan. "I'll tell him to go to hell."

"He'll probably ask you to fire me, Dan."

"So? I'm not going to fire my best reporter."

She grinned, greatly relieved. "I'm also your only reporter."

"Well, all the more reason not to fire you."

"But what if the mayor threatens to go after your advertisers?"

"Look, the Hampton Cove Gazette has been around for over forty years, and will still be here when Mayor Turner is long gone. Politicians have tried to mess with me and my paper before, and failed. My advertisers don't care about politics. They care about having a paper that's widely circulated and popular with its readers, and they know that in order to do that you need ace reporters such as yourself. You just keep doing what you do best, and I'll tell Mayor Turner that he can stick his threats where the sun don't shine."

She smiled at the elderly man. "You're the best, Dan, did you know that?"

"I do, but I don't mind hearing it again from time to time."

"Well, you are."

He spread his arms. "Don't we make a great team? The best editor and the best reporter, annoying the heck out of the celebrities and politicians in this town. Now you go out there and do your thing. You have my blessing."

# CHAPTER 21

$\mathcal{I}$'d decided to take an extended nap, and so had Dooley. After spending all of the previous day out and about, and half the night as well, I was feeling the strain. So today we decided to take a break. If Brutus wanted to traipse around town all day, that was his business, but we were going to sleep.

Odelia had left early that morning, promising she was fine without us for a day. She was going to interview some more people, and if she needed help she'd let us know. So when suddenly a grating voice sounded right next to me, I figured it was Odelia. "All right, all right," I muttered. "One minute."

As usual I took up one half of the couch in Odelia's living room and Dooley the other half. I'd been dreaming of little tweety birds sitting in a tree, and Princess and I had just chased them to the top branch. We were both perched on that branch like Kate and Leo in Titanic, and I was yelling "I'm the king of the world!" when someone said, "I need your help, Maxie, baby."

Only one cat called me Maxie baby, and suddenly my

dream turned into a nightmare. A thump on my shoulder told me this wasn't a dream at all, but brutal reality. And when I opened my eyes and found myself staring into the face of Brutus, I groaned. "Oh, go away," and closed my eyes again.

"I need your help. Chase is leaving town and so am I if I don't stop him."

A jolt of elation shot through me. Had I heard this right? Was Brutus leaving town. "You're leaving?" I asked, sitting bolt upright now.

"Yeah," he said, looking none too pleased.

I saw that Harriet was seated next to him, and it was obvious she'd been crying. Dooley, now coming out of his slumber, muttered, "Who's leaving?"

"Brutus," I told him.

"Hey, that's great," he said blithely. "So when is he going?"

"This isn't funny, Dooley," said Harriet between two sniffs. "Chase resigned. The chief didn't want to fire him but he resigned himself."

"Yeah, we were there when it happened. Right outside the window."

"What happened?" I asked, genuinely interested now.

"It was that horrible drug dealer Chase caught yesterday," Brutus said.

"Odelia caught that drug dealer, not Chase," I corrected him.

"Yeah, yeah, whatever. The creep filed charges for police harassment, and his lawyer must have talked to the Commissioner, Chase's former boss, and he talked to the mayor of this crappy little town and forced the Chief's hand."

"Only Chief Alec refused to fire Chase so Chase decided to quit," Harriet said. "Such an honorable man. And now he's being pressured to leave."

I scratched my head. "That's… surprising." I wondered

what Odelia would have to say about this. She and Chase hadn't exactly hit it off, though I had the impression she was warming to the guy. And now he was leaving. So was this a good thing or a bad thing? Hard to know for sure. My first instinct was to applaud this outcome, since it meant we'd never see Brutus again.

"It gets worse," now a voice spoke from the door. I'd been so focused on Brutus's story I hadn't heard Odelia walk in, but when she took a seat on the couch, between Dooley and me, I could see she wasn't in the best of moods.

"Worse?" cried Harriet. "Oh, no!"

"I just interviewed Veronica George and her mother, Bryony Pistol, Johnny's wife, and I'm convinced that Veronica is behind this whole thing. I think she's the one who called the Commissioner and got Chase to quit."

In a few brief words, she gave us the gist of her interview.

"So you think Veronica and that dealer are still an item?" I asked.

"I'm sure they are. And the more I think about it, the more I'm starting to suspect they might be involved in Johnny's murder."

"But why would Veronica kill her own father?" asked Brutus.

"Money," she said simply. "Johnny was divorcing Bryony so he could marry Jasper, which meant Veronica would lose a big chunk of her inheritance, since the bulk of the estate would go to Jasper in case something happened to Johnny. If she killed him before the divorce was final, Bryony inherited everything, and by extension Veronica. So that's motive for you."

Brutus thought about this for a moment. "You might be right."

"Veronica and Donovan Rubb could easily have set this up together," Odelia continued. "To get his hands on spider venom was a piece of cake for the drug dealer, as he must have all kinds of shady contacts."

"But what about Jasper's fingerprints?" asked Harriet.

She shook her head. "Somehow they must have planted those prints on that vial. I don't know how, but that's the only explanation." She turned to me. "What I want you guys to do is spy on Veronica and Rubb. I want to catch those two together. If I can prove they never broke up, in spite of what Veronica says, maybe I can pressure them into confessing to the murder."

"All right," I agreed immediately. I'd had my nap, so I was good to go.

"Sure thing, toots," said Brutus, and I winced.

Odelia smiled down at the black cat. "So are you guys all working together now? That's a first."

"I don't want to leave this town," Brutus admitted. "I like it here. I've found some great friends…" He gave me a poke in the gut. "And even my sweetheart…" He winked at Harriet. "And Chase likes it here, too."

Odelia nodded. "It's not fair for him to lose his job over these false charges. We have to set the record straight and clear his name once and for all."

"I caught him packing just now," Brutus said. "And I overheard him talking to a friend on the phone about a job in private security, which is just a shame. He loves being a cop. It's all he ever wanted to be. And now this…"

Odelia was right. It wasn't fair. Even though I wasn't a fan of Brutus, we had to make this right, even if it meant having the brute around for a while longer. Or maybe even indefinitely. So I decided to make the big sacrifice.

"We'll help you save your human's career," I told Brutus.

"Thanks, Maxie, baby," said Brutus, and I could see that he meant it.

# CHAPTER 22

For the occasion, Odelia decided to outfit us all with tracking devices. She'd gotten those online a while back, after watching a documentary about a research team following a bunch of cats around for a couple of nights, to see what they were up to. Track their nocturnal wanderings around the small town where they lived. So Odelia had bought us trackers so she'd know where we were at all times. Combined with a panic button, we could send her a signal, and she could come and find us wherever we were holed up.

It was a neat system, and we'd tested it out around the house but had never used it on a mission before. She quickly outfitted the four of us with trackers and panic buttons, both attached to our collars, and then we were all set. I had to hand it to Odelia: when she got mad, she got even. It would be a lesson for Veronica George: never mess with a small-town reporter.

Odelia dropped us off at the house where Veronica lived with her mother, and parked her car around the corner. If she was right, and the woman was still involved with that lowlife drug dealer, it wouldn't be hard for us to catch the two of them together. Then all we had to do was press our buttons.

When the four of us trudged up the driveway, we were almost flattened by a Mercedes GLS driving off and spraying us with gravel. I caught a glimpse of the driver and thought it just might be Veronica, which meant we'd already lost her. Luckily Harriet had jumped to the other side of the car and said, "It was Bryony Pistol. I recognized her from the pictures."

Hand it to Harriet. She's a regular *Star, US Weekly* and *People* reader.

"Great. Let's hope her daughter decided to stay home," I said.

The four of us followed the driveway, which led around the house, and found ourselves in a large flower garden extending into a pool area similar to Johnny's, only smaller. Stretched out on a pool chair was a young woman reading a copy of *Star*, the cover announcing lots of 'Stars Without Makeup.'

"That's Veronica!" hissed Harriet.

She was dressed in a pink bikini, sunglasses perched on her nose, and looked bored. So we hunkered down in the bushes, and took turns watching the pop singer's daughter. Being a private investigator is all about the stakeout, Odelia had once told me, and this prolonged vigil proved her right.

Soon it wasn't just Veronica who looked bored, but us, too.

"So you still believe a conspiracy of escorts killed Johnny?" Dooley asked Brutus.

"Right," I said with a smile. "The Australian boy toy conspiracy. I'd almost forgotten about that."

"I have to admit Odelia's theory is pretty sound, too," said Brutus, idly toying with a beetle. "And it fits right in with my boy toy conspiracy theory."

"Toy boy," murmured Harriet, who'd closed her eyes.

"Whatever," grunted Brutus. "That's the difference between a true detective like myself and amateurs like you and Dooley, Maxie. A true detective comes up with new theories all the time, then checks them against the facts and either discards them or expounds on them. Is it possible a conspiracy of Australian boy toys killed Johnny? Sure. Do the facts bear out this theory? They might, if Chase had been allowed to carry on his work."

I frowned. "So what you're saying is that there's a conspiracy to remove Chase from his job to prevent him from uncovering the truth?"

"A conspiracy to protect a conspiracy," said Dooley. "My mind is officially blown."

"Look, this Veronica chick and that drug guy conspired to remove Chase from the investigation to protect the conspiracy of Australian boy toys."

"Do you know how crazy that sounds?" I asked.

"That's your problem, Maxie, baby. You don't have what it takes to be a truly great detective. You lack imagination."

"So we're conspiring to end the conspiracy that's designed to protect the conspiracy," muttered Dooley. "Wicked."

"See?" asked Brutus. "Your buddy Dooley gets it."

"You're so clever, Brutus," said Harriet. "The smartest cat I know."

"Sure, sure," he said. "C'mere, babe."

And before long they were exchanging kisses, Harriet giggling wildly.

"Oh, please kill me now," Dooley sighed.

Because I didn't want to watch Brutus and Harriet, I stared out at Veronica instead, but as far as I could see nothing was happening with her. She'd picked up another magazine, this one promising to expose Kim Kardashian's beauty secrets, and from time to time she picked up her phone and tapped the screen, presumably texting her friends.

"How long is this going to take?" asked Brutus, when he and Harriet had tired of their frolicking.

"See, this is the reality of being a true detective," I told the black cat. "Waiting around for hours and hours, hoping something will happen."

"And hours and hours," said Dooley.

"Booooring," Brutus grunted. "What about some action? A car chase?"

"There are no car chases in a detective's life," I said. "This isn't *Die Hard*, Brutus, and you're not Bruce Willis."

"Did you know I was named after Bruce? True story."

"You were named after Brutus," I said. "Not Bruce."

"Brutus, Bruce, same difference."

"There is a difference. Brutus was a Roman senator who conspired to kill Caesar, while Bruce is an actor known for—"

"Shush," said Brutus.

I reared up. "Don't shush me, Brutus."

"Shush," he repeated, and gestured at Veronica. I looked over and saw that she'd gotten up, texting furiously, and was walking toward the house.

"Something's happening," Brutus said.

"Very astute of you."

"Probably went to fetch another magazine," muttered Dooley.

But when Veronica didn't return it was obvious something was up.

"We have to see what's going on," I said. "Which means taking a closer look."

"Why don't we send in a volunteer?" Brutus suggested. "I mean, if the four of us all go over there together it will look suspicious, right?"

In spite of myself, I had to agree he had a point.

"All right. I'll go," I said.

"No, I'll go," he said. "It's my human that needs saving, so I should go."

"Yes, but I know how to sneak up on someone without being seen."

"And I don't?" he scoffed. "I'm the best sneaker-upper around, buddy. Just watch me sneak." And before I could stop him, he was off and away, sneaking toward the house, doing his best to keep his belly low to the flagged terrace, his tail down and his ears flat. He looked absolutely ridiculous.

"Doesn't he look wonderful?" gushed Harriet. "A true detective."

"Not really," said Dooley.

Harriet turned on him. "What's with all the criticism, huh? You can't say one good word about Brutus, while he's the most wonderful cat I know."

"So of all the cats you know, he's the best?" asked Dooley, annoyed.

"Yes, he is."

"Greater than all the cats you've ever known? Cats you've lived with all your life? Cats like Max… and me?"

She hesitated, but then said, "Brutus is different."

"Oh, I'll say he's different."

"See?" she said. "Again with the criticism. You're my friend, Dooley, so why can't you simply be happy for me? Happy that I found my soulmate?"

He shrugged. "I am happy for you."

"You don't sound happy."

I grinned when Dooley made a face behind Harriet's back. Then I returned my attention to Brutus, who'd now reached the house and was sneaking inside, still staying low, even though anyone could spot a black cat against white pavement. Suddenly he popped his head back out and waved us over frantically. "We better get over there," I said, quite needlessly.

"She's leaving!" he cried when we'd joined him.

I darted a look inside, and saw he was right: Veronica, now talking animatedly into her phone, had pulled on jeans shorts and a crop top and snatched a small clutch from the table before walking out of the living room.

We quickly hurried out and followed the driveway back to the front of the house, just in time to see a taxi pull up and Veronica get in.

"What do we do now?" asked Harriet, panicking.

"Relax, toots," said Brutus. "We just press this nifty button and warn Odelia that our target is on the move."

"She'll never get here in time," I told him. "One of us has to follow that cab."

"I'll do it," said Brutus. "Just like Bruce, right?"

But while we were holding a strategy meeting, the taxi was already pulling away, so in a spur of the moment kind of thing, I broke into a run.

"Hey, where are you going?!" Brutus cried.

While the car picked up speed, I jumped up onto the trunk, then onto the roof, and grasped the antenna and held on for dear life.

"Press that button!" I yelled, since I couldn't reach it now.

"Maxie, baby!" cried Brutus. "Don't let go!"

Well, that was certainly my intention. Maybe Brutus was right after all. Sometimes being a true detective is a little bit like being Bruce in *Die Hard*.

The taxi took us to the outskirts of town, and soon I saw where we were going: the strip mall where Rubb's health food store was located. He pulled up right in front of the now closed shop, and Veronica got out of the cab.

Relieved we'd finally stopped moving, I managed to crawl down from the roof. My hair was a mess, and I think I'd swallowed more bugs than the windshield on a sixteen-ton truck. If this was what it was like to be Bruce, Brutus was welcome to him.

Veronica checked left and right, and then, to my surprise, disappeared inside the shop, which seemed to be open for business after all. But then, as I watched, an unseen hand quickly turned the sign from 'Open' to 'Closed.'

Since I couldn't follow her inside, I decided to walk around back. I soon found that the backside of these shops was even dingier than the front, and when I'd finally located the one that belonged to The Vitamin King, I selected an oil drum for my own and hopped on top of it. Grimy windows looked out across a junk-littered, weed-infested patch of yard, and I didn't see much at first. But then, as I pressed my nose up against the pane, I saw I was just in time to witness the teary reunion scene between the two lovers. Bingo.

I smiled. So much for a restraining order. There was little restraint when Veronica threw herself into Rubb's arms and kissed him passionately.

# CHAPTER 23

$\mathcal{O}$delia had parked her pickup around the corner from Bryony Pistol's place while her feline detectives did their thing. During the long wait, she'd sat in the backseat, working on her article, pecking away at her laptop. It all fit. Veronica must have heard from her mother that Johnny was going to divorce her and marry Jasper, and she must have decided she had to do away with her father to make sure his large fortune came her way one day, and not Jasper's. With the help of her lover, she'd planted that vial, and had somehow managed to get Jasper's prints on it, to cast the blame on him.

She'd also made sure there was absolutely nothing to connect her to Rubb, even going so far as to file a restraining order and make sure she wasn't seen with him. Which meant she and Rubb must have devised this plan months ago. When she moved to Hampton Cove, Rubb had simply done the same, quickly becoming Johnny's go-to guy for everything drug-related.

What an utterly devious couple, she thought bitterly.

When the signal came, she jumped, and stared at her

smartphone screen. The signal was confusing: three dots were stationary in front of the house, while a fourth dot, Max's, was moving at a fast clip. She decided to pick up Harriet, Dooley and Brutus and then follow Max to wherever he was going.

The moment she stopped in front of the house, Brutus, Harriet and Dooley all started yelling simultaneously. The gist of it was that Max was now clutching to a taxi for dear life, while it carted Veronica away.

"Follow that cab!" Dooley finally managed. He turned to the others. "I've always wanted to say that."

"Good for you," said Brutus, hopping into the pickup. He appeared disgruntled, and probably annoyed he wasn't the one clutching that cab.

So she followed that cab, and it took her to the strip mall and the health food store where she and Chase had caught Rubb the day before.

When she drew near, she saw that the small dot indicated that Max was at the back of The Vitamin King, so she parked her car and carefully made her way over there, the three cats in her wake, like a regular Nancy Drew.

"This is so exciting!" cried Harriet.

"Yeah, like being in an action movie," grunted Brutus.

The stores all had small paved backyards, where the owners collected garbage and smoked a cigarette while on a break. It didn't take them long to find the backyard that belonged to Rubb's business, especially since a large red cat was perched on an oil drum and peering in through the window.

"Hey, Max," she whispered, sneaking up to the ginger tabby.

Max gave a violent start, and practically toppled off the drum.

"You scared the bejesus out of me," he growled. Then he

gestured to the window. "They're in there, and they're showing very little restraint!"

"Great," she said, glad that her hunch had proved correct. She slowly craned her neck, her smartphone at the ready, and saw that Max was right: the kissing couple were obviously very happy to see each other. She quickly snapped a few shots, figuring she'd blur out the nekkid bits later in Photoshop. Readers of the Gazette didn't like their stories X-rated.

"Gotcha," she muttered.

The three other cats now also joined Max on that oil drum, and this proved to be their downfall. Literally. The oil drum suddenly pitched, and then clattered to the ground with a terrible clanking sound. Uh-oh. She ducked down immediately, but too late. The window above her was pushed open, and Donovan Rubb's perfectly bearded face appeared. When he caught sight of her, he shouted, "You again!"

She gave him a cheery wave from her vantage point. "Hi, there, Donny."

But instead of returning her greeting, he suddenly latched onto her smartphone, which she was clutching in her hand, and gave her a push.

"Hey! That's mine!" she yelled as she fell backward.

"And now it's mine!" he yelled back, and then disappeared.

She quickly scrambled to her feet, but by the time she was at the window again, Rubb was gone, and so was Veronica. Great. She lost them.

"This is so déjà-vu!" she groaned.

She retraced her steps, four cats on her heels, but when she arrived at her car she saw that Rubb was already straddling his trusty red Ducati—probably fresh from the police impound—and Veronica was wrapping herself around him on the pillion. They were going to make a run for it. Of course.

She raced to her pickup, but by the time she was behind the wheel, the Ducati was already speeding away. She held the door for the four cats, who piled in behind her, and then she slammed the door, shoved the car in gear and was off behind the fleeing Bonnie and Clyde.

As she raced after the Ducati, her mind flashed back to the previous day, when she'd gone through this exact same experience, only with Chase by her side. And suddenly she felt a little melancholic. Whatever his faults, Chase was a great cop, and he would be missed in this town. No, she had to admit, actually she'd miss him. How crazy was that?

Just like the day before, Rubb took the road through town, and once again, she lagged behind, dodging pedestrians and making sure she didn't clip anybody while he simply zigzagged through traffic and was soon a blip on the horizon. Once she'd cleared the city limits, she picked up speed, pushing the aged truck to its limits, and had soon caught up with the Ducati.

"Pull over!" she shouted when she came up next to the couple.

"Never!" Rubb shouted back.

"Back off, bitch!" Veronica screamed.

She gritted her teeth, resisting a strong urge to send the bike into the ditch again, but then soon found she didn't have to, as Brutus suddenly launched himself out of the passenger window and latched onto Rubb's face, his claws finding purchase on the hipster dealer's beard!

Rubb screamed a very unmanly scream when suddenly he found his vision impaired by ten inches of black cat and his face used as a pincushion. The Ducati sailed straight into the ditch, sending Rubb and Veronica flying.

Odelia brought her pickup to a stop and quickly jumped

out to assess the damage. To her surprise, she saw that Brutus was still stuck to Rubb's face, like the Facehugger from Alien, refusing to let go. Both Rubb and Veronica were howling, though Rubb's howls sounded a little muffled.

"I think you can let go now, Brutus," said Odelia, and the cat did, immediately starting to lick his paws to remove the stench of human.

"Yippee-ki-yay, asshole," he said with a Cheshire grin.

# CHAPTER 24

It was a pity Chase wasn't there to outfit Veronica and her drug dealer boyfriend with a nice set of handcuffs, but since they both looked pretty banged up, and Rubb's Ducati looked like a total loss, Odelia didn't think they'd skedaddle this time. She sat cross-legged across from the couple.

"So what about that restraining order, huh?" she asked Veronica. "Looks like it didn't restrain you from going near this freak."

"Hey, that's Mr. Freak to you," grunted Rubb.

She'd retrieved her phone from the dealer, who now sat spitting out cat hair and checking his face for puncture holes. She leafed through the snapshots she'd taken of the couple.

"Pretty hot," she said as she held out her phone so they could have a peek. "I wonder what my uncle will say when he sees these. Oh, I know. He'll say that the two of you planned the murder of John Paul George together. Who was the brains behind the operation? I'll go out on a limb here and say that it was you, Veronica. The doting daughter?"

"You think I killed my father? You're even crazier than I thought."

"Well, I also thought you and lover boy over here were still seeing each other, so not so crazy after all." She pointed an accusing finger at Veronica, whose tank top was on backward. In her haste to get dressed, she'd missed that minor detail. Like her boyfriend, she looked a little frazzled, and was now checking a broken fingernail. No other bones were broken, though.

"I have nothing to say to you," she said.

"That's all right. I have plenty to say to you. You weren't happy about Johnny divorcing your mother and marrying Jasper, which would make you lose out on several hundred million dollars, so you figured you'd better kill him now before it was too late. So you asked your boyfriend to supply the venom—where did you get that, Donny? I guess a man with your contacts would have no trouble acquiring that kind of stuff, huh? And then somehow you managed to get Jasper's fingerprints on the vial to make him take the fall and voila. Easy peasy. Now all you needed to do was make sure that there was no connection between you and Donny, so you faked a breakup, which I'm sure made your mother happy, and even went so far as to get a restraining order."

"All lies," said Veronica, but she looked like the fight had left her. She knew that Odelia was holding all the cards now, with those pictures of her.

"Tell her about Chase," Brutus supplied helpfully. "How she set him up."

"And then there's that little matter of Chase Kingsley," said Odelia.

"What about him?"

"He never did assault you, did he? You just made that up because Commissioner Necker asked you to. You cut a deal so Donny would walk free, in exchange for your testimony against Detective Kingsley."

Veronica was giving her just about the meanest look any woman had ever given her, but Odelia didn't care. She had proof, and she wasn't letting go.

She tapped her phone. "You know what I'll do? I'll publish these on the front page of tomorrow's Hampton Cove Gazette. Let the good people of this town draw their own conclusions. I'll blur out the X-rated parts, of course. Don't want to shock people more than is strictly necessary."

"You can't do that," said Veronica hoarsely. She looked appalled.

"I can and I will," she promised.

"Look, I didn't kill my father, all right?" said Veronica. "I would never do that. I loved that man. He was a deeply flawed individual, but he was also a very sweet guy. The problem was that he had the mental age of a fifteen-year-old, which made me feel like I was dealing with a younger brother, not a father. I still loved him, though, like the funny, goofy guy he was. And as far as money is concerned, he set up a trust fund in my name when I was born. I don't know how much is in there but last time I checked there were millions. So it's not exactly as if I'm hard up or anything. And I was happy for Jasper. He's more mature than my dad ever was, and he was like a second father to me. He deserved everything that was coming to him, including the wedding. It wasn't easy being Dad's significant other—just ask my mom. Jasper had to make a lot of sacrifices over the years, and I didn't begrudge him anything."

"Millions of dollars?" asked Rubb, eyes wide. "So you're loaded, babe?"

She smiled. "Pretty much. I didn't want to tell you as I was afraid you'd only like me for my money and not for me."

"You told me the only money you had was your allowance."

"Which is probably more than you've made in your entire life."

He whistled through his teeth. "Well, I'll be damned, babe."

"Look, what about the poison?" Odelia asked, not liking the direction this conversation was taking. Veronica should be confessing by now, but instead she was making a pretty convincing case she was innocent in JPG's murder.

"What poison?" asked Veronica with a frown.

"The spider venom. The only one who could have supplied that was your boyfriend."

"Hey, don't look at me, crazy lady," said Rubb. "Like I told you yesterday, I had nothing to do with that spider stuff. I might be able to get my hands on some top quality narcotics, but I don't know the first thing about some weird spider venom. Besides, why would I kill my best customer? That's just crazy."

"Because you wanted to help your girlfriend vouchsafe her inheritance."

"I didn't even know she was loaded, all right? She never told me."

"And with good reason," Veronica said. "Now I know you love me for me, and not for my money."

"I've always loved you for you, babe."

"Listen, what about Chase Kingsley?" asked Odelia, who hated to admit she was starting to believe these two were innocent after all.

Veronica hesitated. "If I tell you what happened, do you promise to delete those pictures? I so don't want them on the Internet. I'd die of shame."

"I promise not to publish them. I'll keep them, though. Just in case."

"All right. Yes, I did lie about Detective Kingsley."

"Don't tell her that, babe. They might put me back in prison."

"No, they won't," she said. "This time I'm getting you the best lawyer money can buy, whatever Mom says. And I'm going to tell her everything."

"Why don't you begin by telling me everything?" Odelia asked.

"You were right," said Veronica. "I set up Detective Kingsley because Commissioner Necker made a deal. In exchange for Donny walking free, all charges dropped, I had to make up a story about Detective Kingsley harassing me. I filed those charges and that restraining order, just like he asked me to, and the next thing I knew, Donny was sprung from prison."

"Did the Commissioner tell you what it was all about?"

She shook her head. "I never spoke with Commissioner Necker himself. Everything was arranged through Donny's lawyer, who swore us to secrecy."

"And a lousy lawyer he was."

"Mom forbade me to get a decent one, so this one was all we had," Veronica explained. "I'm pretty sure he was working for the Commissioner all along. They just needed someone to agree to do the dirty on Kingsley."

"Will you retract your statement?"

"I will," she said.

"Why the restraining order against Donny?" she asked.

She rolled her eyes. "That was Mother's idea. She'd seen how easy it was to get one against Kingsley, so she told me to get one against Donny. She'd never liked him."

"That woman hates me," grunted Rubb, waggling his beard indignantly.

"What's not to like?" asked Odelia. "Having a drug dealer for a son-in-law is probably every mother's dream."

"She's right, you know," said Veronica. "You have to stop with that drug business, babe. It's going to get you killed one of these days."

"Not to mention a bunch of other people," said Odelia, shaking her head.

"I know," he grumbled. "But it's easy money. And everybody loves my product. You wouldn't believe how popular I am amongst the celebrity set."

"Did you move out here to be closer to Veronica?" asked Odelia.

"Yes, I did," he said, pulling her close and planting a kiss on the tip of her nose. "I already had a few high-profile customers back in New York, so it wasn't hard to make the move, as a lot of them had a weekend place out here. And when Veronica introduced me to her dad, I knew I had a winner."

"I only did that to make sure Dad had the best quality drugs," said Veronica with a shrug. "If he was going to take that stuff anyway, he might as well buy from Donny." She tapped his nose. "But now you're through."

"If you say so," he grumbled.

"Yes, I do. If Mother is ever going to accept you, you need to go legit."

"You're going to introduce me to your mom again?"

"I am. And this time she's going to accept you. Just you wait and see."

Rubb didn't look too happy about that prospect, but Odelia had the impression that Veronica was the type of woman who liked to get her way, and she was pretty sure she was going to see this through. She didn't like her cavalier attitude toward drugs, but at least she'd come clean about Chase.

"So we have a deal?" she asked. "You're retracting your statement about Chase Kingsley?"

"Yes," said Veronica. "And you promise never to publish those pictures?"

"Deal," said Odelia, and they shook hands on it. In one fell swoop she'd rid Hampton Cove of a drug dealer, and Chase Kingsley of his pesky accuser. She'd also lost a perfectly good suspect in Johnny's murder, but that couldn't be helped. She believed Veronica. She hadn't killed her father. So who had?

## CHAPTER 25

*A*fter she'd dropped the couple off at Veronica's place, Odelia drove to her uncle's house to give Chase the good news. When she arrived, she found the back door open, as usual. Alec didn't believe in locking his door, figuring nobody would be so stupid to break into the house of the chief of police.

She walked through the kitchen, which was squeaky clean. Her uncle never cooked, and neither did Chase, apparently. All she found were two cups in the sink and half a pot of cold coffee in the coffeemaker.

She went upstairs to look for Chase, taking the stairs two at a time.

"Chase? Are you up there?"

"Over here," he bellowed, and she found him in the guest bedroom, his suitcase open on the bed, while he was seated next to it, staring at a picture frame of an older man in police uniform. He looked like Chase, but older.

"Your dad?" she guessed.

He looked up. "Yeah, this was taken when he got a

commendation." He dumped the picture frame on top of his luggage.

"I've got some great news for you," she said, grabbing a chair.

"Oh? What's that?"

She quickly told him the story of what had transpired just now, and his eyebrows raised a fraction of an inch.

"So Veronica George finally decided to come clean, huh? Well done."

"I just thought you'd like to know she's going to retract her statement, so you should be good to stay on here in Hampton Cove. I'm sure my uncle will take you back in a heartbeat."

"Too late," he said, surprising her.

"Too late? What do you mean? This is your chance, Chase."

He gave her a weary look. "My reputation is shot to hell, Odelia. Even if Veronica retracts her statement, those rumors will never go away. Not until the whole story comes out, and even then they'll persist. It's like with those apologies the tabloids publish in small print on the bottom of page fifty after they've destroyed your reputation on the front page just days before."

"This won't be buried on page fifty, Chase. I'll get you the front page."

He shook his head. "Muds sticks, Odelia. No matter what you write."

"Not when I reveal the truth and do the whole story, like you said."

He raked his fingers through his hair. "What are you going to write?"

"I'll print the retraction on the front page. Clear your name entirely."

"Like I said, mud sticks. I can't be a cop in this town, not with half the population believing I'm dirty. I'll never have the authority I need again."

"But—"

He held up his hand to silence her. "Look, I appreciate what you've done for me, I really do, but my mind is made up. This part of my life is over."

She stared at him, defeated. "What are you going to do?"

"A buddy of mine set up his own business in Cleveland. Private security. He's always asked me to join him so I finally told him I would. It's not as much fun as being a cop, but it's a paycheck."

She stared at the picture frame of Chase's dad. "Is that what your dad would have wanted? You running away like this?"

For a moment, the fire returned to his eyes. "I'm not running away. I just know when it's time to call it quits. And right now it's time to move on."

She remembered something Brutus said. "Wasn't being a cop your dream?"

He stared at her. "Yes, it was. My dad was a cop, so naturally I thought being a cop was the greatest thing ever. And it was. It still is."

She realized she didn't know Chase all that well. In the short time he'd been here, he'd made quite an impression on her, but he'd never discussed his personal life.

"Your dad… is he retired now?"

"Retired to that big old retirement home in the sky," said Chase.

"Oh… I'm so sorry, Chase."

"One week before his retirement he broke up a fight on the Lower East Side. Some dumb dispute about a hot dog stand. One guy suddenly took out a gun and fired off a warning shot. The shot went wide and hit my dad in the carotid artery and he bled to death. Dumbest death ever."

"Oh, God, Chase. That's horrible."

"Mom didn't take it too well, as you can imagine. She hasn't been the same since. The fact that her son was kicked off the force didn't help either."

"Where is she now?"

"Living with her sister in the Bronx. I'd take her, but I'm not exactly in a position to do so right now."

"But don't you want to stay close? Ohio is a long way from your family."

He shrugged. "It's a job. A man's got to eat."

"Look, what if I expose the Commissioner? Would that help?"

He stared at her. "And how exactly are you going to do that?"

"I have my sources. I'll figure something out."

"You can't go throwing out wild accusations, Odelia. They'll come after you next. This guy… he's ruthless. And it's not just the Commissioner, you're going up against the mayor as well. Both powerful men, both trying to protect their careers now that there are important elections coming up."

"I'm a big girl, Chase. I can handle myself," she promised him.

He gave her a grimace. "You better have ironclad proof, or else they're going to sink your career like they sank mine. In fact I'd advise you to stay away from this whole business." He rose from the bed, grasped her hand and shook it. "See you around, Odelia Poole. It was nice sparring with you."

"I'm not giving up on this yet," she said adamantly. "This town needs a good cop like you, Chase, and I'm going to make sure you stick around."

He shook his head. "Keep dreaming, Poole."

"That's exactly what I'm going to do." She wasn't doing this for herself. She was doing this for Chase, for his mother, and for Hampton Cove. Because this town deserved a great cop like him, and his mother deserved a break, and so did he. The fact that her heart suddenly hurt when she thought about him leaving town never to return had nothing to do with it, of course.

## CHAPTER 26

*W*hen Odelia walked back to the car, she was looking disappointed. It was obvious her one-on-one with Chase hadn't gone as well as she'd hoped.

"What?" asked Brutus eagerly. "Is he staying?"

She shook her head as she slipped behind the wheel. "No. He says he's moving to Cleveland, to start working private security with a buddy of his."

"Cleveland? Where is Cleveland?" asked Harriet.

"Ohio," I told her.

"Where's Ohio?" asked Dooley.

"Far away from here," said Odelia, clearly not too happy.

"But didn't you tell him about Veronica?" cried Brutus, dismayed.

"I did," she said, slumping behind the wheel. "He said it's too little too late. His reputation is shot to hell, and people won't trust him as a cop."

"Like trying to put toothpaste back into the tube," I said.

"Exactly," said Odelia with a wan smile. "Thanks for that imagery, Max."

"It's not so hard to put toothpaste back into the tube," said Dooley.

"No? Let's see you try it," said Odelia.

"You just... do it," said Dooley, sounding like a commercial for Nike.

"Why don't you just write a big, beautiful story on the front page and convince everybody what a magnificent person Chase really is?" asked Harriet, gazing at Brutus as if he was the most magnificent cat she knew.

"Unless I print the whole story, with irrefutable proof, that won't make much of a difference," said Odelia. "No, Chase is right."

"But... that means you're leaving?" Harriet asked Brutus, eyes wide.

Brutus, for the first time since I'd met him, looked crestfallen. "Oh, tootsie roll," he croaked.

"Oh, honey pie," she whispered, and they both broke into tears. It was a little pathetic, but also heartbreaking.

"Look, I promised Chase I'd break the story of the Commissioner's dirty little secret," said Odelia, turning to me, "but I need your help. I need to have positive proof of this affair. Without that, we're sunk. It's Chase's word against the Commissioner's, and we all know who the public will believe."

I thought about this for a moment, then I nodded. "I think I know just the cat to talk to."

"Well, you go do that, and I'll..." She waved her hands helplessly. "I need to rethink this entire murder thing. If Veronica didn't do it, and neither did Jasper... Well, then I really don't know who did," she finished.

"Can you drop us off at the mall?" I asked, and even though she eyed me curiously, she didn't ask why. She drove us over and let us out of the car.

"Do you need me to pick you up later on?" she asked,

gesturing at the tracker and panic button combo that was still fastened to my collar.

"Yes, that would be great," I said. We'd been traipsing around so much I was starting to feel the strain.

"So where are we going?" asked Dooley when Odelia had left.

I motioned to a small collection of dumpsters across the parking lot from the strip mall. "Where do you think?"

He stared at the dumpsters. "Are you hungry? If you are, you should have asked Odelia to drop us off at Johnny's place. I'm sure Princess and George wouldn't mind sharing their food with us again. They've got plenty."

"We're not here to eat, Dooley," I said. "We're here to talk to a certain individual who's usually very well-informed and might be able to help us."

He frowned. "You mean that bearded hipster drug dealer?"

"Not him," I said as I set paw for the dumpsters. Brutus and Harriet were lagging behind, still consoling each other and coming to terms with their imminent breakup. It broke my heart to see them, and I had to admit I just might have misjudged Brutus. To look as brokenhearted as he did, it meant he really cared about Harriet, which meant that he actually had a warm heart beating beneath that rugged exterior of his and not just a solid block of ice.

We arrived at the dumpsters. It was here that the shops comprising the mall dumped their trash, and it also served as a place where all manner of vermin gathered. Not just critters favored this place, though, but also one of Hampton Cove's most feral feline inhabitants. She lived out in the woods, near the old hunting lodge that was now the Writer's Lodge, where best-selling and not-so-best-selling writers came to write in all peace and quiet.

A murder had taken place there last year, and Clarice, the

cat I was hoping to meet, had helped us solve it. She belonged to no one and got her food all over the place, so she was the right cat to ask if she knew how to catch Commissioner Necker and Mayor Putin's wife in the act. It was a long shot, but it was the only thing I could think of. We were all out of options, and if we were going to keep Chase around, we had to go for broke.

"Clarice," I called out. "Are you here? It's Max."

"Clarice?" asked Brutus. "Who's Clarice?"

"Oh, Clarice!" Dooley cried happily, then his face dropped. "You're not thinking about making another deal with Clarice, are you?" His paw involuntarily reached to his nose and he winced.

The last time we'd talked to the feral cat, she'd made us vow a blood oath, which had involved cutting ourselves and mixing our blood. Only Dooley hadn't been able to cut himself, so Clarice had done the honors and sliced her claws across his nose. I'd been forced to listen to his laments for days.

"What do you want now?" suddenly asked a hollow voice. It seemed to come from all around us, echoing between the dozens of metal dumpsters.

"A friend of ours is in in big trouble!"

"So you've come to ask me for a favor again?" the voice echoed.

"That's right. We need your help, Clarice."

"Yes, Clarice," Harriet chimed in. "We really need your help."

"Who's that?" the voice bellowed.

"My name is Harriet. I'm Marge Poole's Persian? My friend Brutus's human is in trouble."

"Helping humans again, are we?" Clarice growled, not sounding convinced. "When are you finally going to realize you're cats? Cats help themselves! Not humans!"

"Well, we happen to like our humans," said Dooley. "So we like to help them if we can. And in exchange they give us food and shelter and love and cuddles and—"

"Shut up, you make me sick!" Clarice bellowed.

Suddenly there was a loud clanking sound behind us, and the wild cat appeared at the rim of a dumpster, then gracefully jumped to the floor beneath. She had a fishbone stuck to her brow, and Dooley winced. He didn't like Clarice, and he didn't like fish, which was a little strange for a cat.

Clarice was a mangy cat, scrawny and more than a little scary. Her eyes seemed to glow red in the obscurity between the dumpsters, and her claws clicked on the concrete ground. When she spoke, it sounded like a hiss, and she gave the impression she was about to pounce and rip us to shreds.

"What do you want?" she hissed. She wasn't the most pleasant cat to deal with, but because of her peripatetic ways she was unusually well-informed.

I quickly explained the predicament we found ourselves in, and she eyed me stoically all the while. If she knew something, she wasn't letting on.

"I might be able to help you," she finally said, "but what is in it for me?"

"We know a place that serves the most delicious food imaginable," I said. "Actual pâté in an all-you-can-eat buffet. They'll even adopt you if you like."

"Where is this place?" she asked, plucking the fishbone from her brow and throwing it down.

"John Paul George's house," I said. "Xanadu."

"He's not there right now," said Dooley helpfully, "because he's dead, but his boyfriend is. Oh, wait, no. He's in jail for murder. But the food is there. And so are a dozen cats. But they won't bother you," he hurriedly added.

"Pâté, huh?" asked Clarice, her eyes glittering. "I've heard rumors about Xanadu, but I always thought it was just a myth. A folk tale."

"It's not a myth," I told her. "We were there, and we ate that pâté."

"And it was to die for," said Dooley.

Harriet slowly turned to me. "You ate pâté and you didn't tell me?"

"We were there on official cat choir business," I said. "And since you're not in the cat choir…"

"Cat choir?" asked Brutus. "That sounds like something for me."

"Oh, God," groaned Dooley.

"Can you even sing?" I asked. "The first rule of cat choir is—"

"You do not talk about cat choir," Dooley said, eyeing me reproachfully.

"Is that you have to be able to sing," I said, ignoring Dooley's outburst.

"I sing like a nightingale," Brutus grunted. "Listen to this." And he suddenly broke out into a caterwauling the likes of which I'd never heard before—it was truly terrible. Like a cat being castrated without sedation.

"Shut the hell up!" growled Clarice. "If you don't want me to cut you."

Offended, Brutus said, "If you think you can do better…"

"I don't *think* I can do better," Clarice hissed. And at this, she burst into song, belting out an aria from some little-known opera. It sounded… nice.

"Hey, that was great!" cried Dooley. "You have to join the choir!"

"Over my dead body," she grumbled. "I wouldn't be seen dead with a bunch of namby-pamby losers like you."

"You could be our conductor," I said. "We have a conductor now, but she's… not very good." In fact Shanille simply tried to copy her human, Father Reilly, who led the church choir, and did a pretty lousy job as well.

"Enough about the cat choir," she said. "Do you want to know about this cheating commissioner business or not?"

"Yes, please," said Harriet, clutching Brutus's paw. "It's a matter of life and death." She turned to Brutus. "I can't imagine life without you, sweets."

"Aw, sugar pie," said Brutus, touched.

"Enough with this nonsense!" cried Clarice. "I'll take your offer of the Xanadu pâté, but first we need to do the oath."

"Oh, not the oath!" Dooley cried.

"Yes, the oath. I can't tell you about my private affairs unless we all swear an oath to secrecy." She held up her right paw and gave it a quick slit with her left claw. A drop of blood appeared, and suddenly there was a sigh behind me and a dull sound. When I looked, I saw Brutus had collapsed.

"Brutus!" cried Harriet. "Sweetie, baby!"

She managed to revive him while we watched on, and he stared up at us, looking woozy. "Blood," he finally muttered. "Can't stand the sight of it."

"Oh, you bunch of sissies," Clarice growled. "Look, no oath, no information."

"I'll do it for you, my turtle-dove," said Harriet. "You just close your eyes."

Brutus squeezed his eyes tightly shut, and Harriet made a small incision in his paw, then in her own. That only left Dooley and me. I winced when I made the cut, and Dooley… just stood there, lips trembling, eyes locked on Clarice, who was eyeing him grimly.

"Well?" she asked. "What's it gonna be? I haven't got all day."

"Oh, for crying out loud," I grunted, and walked over to him and scratched his nose.

"Ouch!" he cried. "What did you do that for?!"

"Because I know that you don't want to be the one who prevented us from saving Chase!"

"You're dead to me," he said in a whiny voice.

"That's fine with me. Just do it already," I told Clarice.

She held her paw against mine, then Harriet joined in and then Brutus, his eyes still shut tight, and then we all pressed our bloody paws against Dooley's injured nose, who whimpered in pain, even though I can't imagine it could have hurt all that much.

"Wimp," Clarice muttered.

"It hurts!"

"Right," said Clarice, satisfied as we all started licking our paws, and Dooley his nose. "Commissioner Necker and Malka Putin have been using the Writer's Lodge for months now. Since there are no bookings—because of that murdered writer—they've got the place all to themselves, and have been coming out here every weekend. I've seen them at it," she said with a grimace. "And let me tell you, it's not for the faint of heart. I consider myself a pretty tough baby and the way they go on is pretty damn disgusting."

"Sex?" I asked.

"Human sex," she clarified.

"Yuck," I said.

"Tell me about it."

"So are they there right now?" I asked.

She smiled, flashing her razor-sharp teeth. "Oh, yes, they are."

# CHAPTER 27

It is one of those annoying things when a detective comes at the end of her long list of suspects and discovers there aren't any left. Odelia wasn't a detective, per se, but she certainly wanted to catch a killer, and when she stared down at her notebook, she found she'd scratched out all the names. Veronica had been her final and most promising suspect, and now she'd lost her as well. Dang, she thought, as she threw her notebook on the dash.

So now what? Start from scratch?

She stared out through the windshield, gathering her thoughts. After dropping off her litter of cats, she'd idly driven around, trying to gather her thoughts, and now found she'd returned to Bryony Pistol's place. Which was just as well, for she wanted another word with Johnny's widow anyway. Last time she'd practically been shown the door, and she wanted to talk to her a little more about Johnny, and whether the man had any other enemies.

And as she thought some more about this, she found that there were many more suspects to be interviewed: perhaps Johnny's housekeeper had seen something, or his gardener, or his pool boy. And then there were his manager, fellow musicians, perhaps a lawyer… Though she was pretty sure Uncle Alec had covered all his bases and had questioned all those people.

She got out of the car, walked up to the gate and pressed the bell. She just hoped that Bryony wouldn't hold her attitude toward her daughter against her. Maybe she should start by apologizing for her earlier behavior. But the gate immediately swung open, which she took as a good sign, and she took a firmer grip on her clutch and crossed the gravel driveway to the house.

Yellow and gold gravel crunched under her feet, reminding her of the brown sugar she liked to put on her pancakes. There was a small pink fountain in the driveway, a replica of the one in front of Johnny's house, only instead of Johnny spewing out the water, a cherubic angel did the honors.

The moment she arrived at the door, it swung open, revealing Bryony.

"Hi," she said. "Sorry to bother you again, Mrs. Pistol. I wanted to apologize about before, and ask you a few more questions if you don't mind."

"Apology accepted," said the woman curtly. As she led her inside, she said, "You just missed Veronica and… that man. She told me about your incident. And how she decided to come clean about Detective Kingsley."

"Yes, that's right. She told me Detective Kingsley is innocent after all."

They'd arrived in the same parlor where they'd held their earlier interview, and Bryony raised her eyes skyward. "How any child of mine could turn out to be such a liar… and all because of that horrible man."

Bryony took a seat on the red velvet sofa while Odelia took the chair. "He promised me he's out of the drug business. And I happen to believe him."

"Men lie, Miss Poole, and men who use drugs even more. I've seen it with my husband. When we were still together he promised me time and time again he'd quit using, and the moment my back was turned he was at it again. It's a very hard habit to kick, and the last thing I wanted was for my daughter to get involved in the same nasty business that ruined her father."

"At least she's not a user herself," said Odelia.

"No, at least there's that. Thank heaven for small favors. With a father who's a heavy user and a boyfriend who's a dealer that's a small miracle."

"Were you never tempted yourself?"

"Never," said Bryony adamantly. "I witnessed firsthand what drugs did to Johnny. He could have been one of the true greats, and instead he chose to waste his entire life and throw away his unique gift. Such a terrible shame."

"Yes, it is a terrible thing." She looked around the room. It was decorated in a floral motif, both wallpaper and upholstering pink roses on an off-white background. Even the parquet floor was inlaid with a rose motif. Very pretty.

"So what did you want to know?" asked Bryony.

"Well, Veronica told me her father set up a trust fund in her name. So she would never have to worry about money ever again?"

"That's right," she said with a smile. "I told him to, so he did."

"Did he make the same arrangement for you? If I'm being too blunt, just tell me," she quickly added when the woman's face clouded.

"No, that's all right. It's not a great secret. Johnny never saw any reason to set up a trust fund for me, as we never divorced. And as his wife I was entitled to half his fortune in case something ever happened to him."

"And in case he remarried?"

"Well, he said he would take good care of me," the woman said with a tight smile. "Johnny knew he owed me his career, and he wasn't going to leave me penniless. So I'm sure he was going to make some arrangement."

Odelia's eyes darted to a side table carrying at least a dozen framed pictures. Most of them were of Veronica, with one picturing her donning a graduation cap and gown, smiling into the camera. Then she suddenly saw another picture and she blinked, startled. It showed Bryony and looked recent. Very recent. Bryony, who'd followed Odelia's gaze, now rose. "Can I get you something, Miss Poole? Tea, perhaps, or coffee? I just made some."

"Yes, please," she said, nodding distractedly.

She now saw she'd been wrong... about everything.

"Don't go anywhere," said Bryony with a smile, and left the parlor.

She quickly got up and checked the picture more closely. There was no mistaking the background. It was the iconic Sydney opera house, a popular and famous landmark. Suddenly, Bryony's voice sounded behind her. "That was taken last month. I was there to take care of some business for Johnny."

She set a tray of cups and saucers down on the coffee table.

"Last month?" she asked, suddenly feeling a little out of her depth.

Bryony gave a tight smile. "Johnny wanted to relaunch his career. He'd had an offer to join the jury on the Australian version of *The X Factor*. He figured it would give him some much-needed exposure so I went to talk to the producers about his involvement." She absentmindedly brushed a strand of hair from her brow. "In spite of the divorce Johnny insisted I represent him. I don't know why, as he was casting me aside for Jasper, but then Jasper was always more like a glorified butler than a genuine manager."

Odelia swallowed. "You... didn't like Jasper?"

Bryony swept up her hand. "You can drop the charade now, Miss Poole. We both know perfectly well why you're here. I don't know how, but you discovered my little secret, didn't you? You discovered I killed Johnny."

"No, I..." But then she noticed the small revolver in Bryony's hand.

"How did you find out? Was it something I said?" Her eyes quickly cut to the picture. "I should never have left that out in the open."

"You got the venom when you were over there," she said.

"Yes. It wasn't hard. They gave me a tour of one of those reptile parks, and showed me where they kept the venom they collect to create anti-venom. It wasn't difficult for me to grab some and bring it back to the States."

"You do know that spider venom isn't lethal when ingested?"

Bryony stared at her. "What are you talking about? It killed Johnny, didn't it?"

"Only because he had a preexisting heart condition. If he'd been healthy he would have survived."

Bryony gave an annoyed shrug. "Who cares? He's dead, isn't he?"

"But why?" she asked. "Why would you want to kill your husband?"

"Oh, don't pretend you don't know," said Bryony. "I'm sure you figured it all out before you set foot in here. What I don't understand is why you didn't bring your uncle along this time, to place me under arrest. Or perhaps you weren't entirely sure and decided to confront me first?" She waved the gun. "Bad idea, Miss Poole. Very bad idea."

"You're not going to kill me, are you?" she asked, frozen to the spot.

"Move over to the window," Bryony said.

Odelia did as she was told, and saw that a blue tarp was placed between the couch and the window. Oh, God. Bryony *was* going to kill her.

"The painters are coming in tomorrow," Bryony explained. "But they'll just have to find themselves another piece of plastic, won't they?"

"But why?" she asked, tears springing to her eyes.

"Isn't it obvious? You're here to arrest me. And I can't have that."

"I can't arrest you. I'm not a cop."

"You sure act like one. And your uncle seems to consider you his deputy. Did you tell him about me?"

She shook her head, living through this entire scene like a dream. She'd never been threatened before, and definitely not been on the verge of being shot before, and her preservation instincts were decidedly slow to respond to this crisis. "I honestly didn't know you killed Johnny," she said now.

Bryony shrugged. "Doesn't matter. You know now, so I can't let you live."

"But why did you kill him?"

"And here I thought you were so smart. The man was going to divorce me. After all those years he was going to leave me and marry that fool Jasper. After I spent a fortune and my entire life turning him into a star he was going to give me a measly annuity. Not even a lump sum but a paltry allowance."

"You could have gotten a lawyer and gotten a better deal."

"I couldn't. We signed a prenup."

"In Johnny's favor? I thought he was the pauper and you the rich girl?"

Bryony shifted the gun to her other hand. "Nicely put.

And you're right. I was rich and Johnny was poor, which is exactly why my father demanded we sign a prenup. Unfortunately I neglected to include a clause that would grant me a portion of moneys earned during our marriage, only that we'd both get back what we'd put in."

"Which for you was your entire fortune, right?"

"Wrong. I never invested anything. My father did, on my request. Upon divorce, I get back exactly what I put in: nothing. And Johnny gets to keep what he made throughout our marriage. Very unfair, but there you have it."

"So he was going to leave you with an annuity? That seems harsh."

"It was. Since his career was in decline—or in a state of rigor mortis, to be exact—and he spent every cent he owned on his very expensive hobbies, his fortune had dwindled. He'd effectively blown most of my money and his."

"So these songs he'd recorded—"

"Were for his comeback record. Which he hoped would put him back on top. There was still a nice chunk of change left, but he was keeping it."

"And so you decided you needed to kill him now or lose out forever."

She smiled. "You are a great reporter, Miss Poole. Yes, Johnny called me to the house a couple of weeks ago, and said he wanted to marry Jasper. Make things official between them. He wanted a divorce. He said he'd always take care of me, and offered me the annuity scheme." She shook her head. "I was livid. After spending the best years of my life and my family's fortune on this man, he was going to fob me off with a few alms? No way. So I decided to get rid of him before the divorce, and salvage what I could from this mess."

"And get rid of Jasper in the process."

"Of course. I never liked that horrid little man. Jail is too good for him."

"So how did you do it?" She needed to buy time. Time to find a solution.

"Well, I thought long and hard about a way to kill the bastard. It's not easy to kill a person and get away with it if you've never done it before." She sounded bemused now, as if the entire murder proposition had been nothing but an intriguing puzzle to her. "I thought about an overdose, which would have looked plausible, but Johnny was always very careful about his dope. The idea came to me when I was in Australia. Some news segment about a boy who'd been bitten by the world's deadliest spider. As luck would have it, they invited me to visit the reptile center and that's where I got the venom."

"But how did you get Jasper's fingerprint on the vial?"

She waved a hand. "I'd seen that on a crime show. I used a piece of tape to lift Jasper's prints from a wine glass when I was over at Johnny's house, and attach them to the vial. It was actually a lot easier than I thought."

"Clever," said Odelia.

"Yes, the plan was very straightforward and easy," said Bryony, "which told me it was the right thing to do. Now all I need to do is get rid of you."

"My uncle will come looking. He'll know what you did."

"I don't think so, hon. I'll just get rid of your car and the body and your uncle will simply think you skedaddled."

"I would never do that."

"Well, you're going to." She raised the gun. "Please lie down, Miss Poole. I don't want any blood on my curtains. I like my murders nice and tidy."

# CHAPTER 28

*B*ryony took careful aim, and it was obvious she knew how to handle a gun. Odelia had done as instructed and was now lying on the tarp, awaiting the end. She thought about rushing the woman and slapping that gun from her hand, but Bryony was no fool. She kept her distance. Besides, chances were that the moment she made a move the woman would shoot anyway.

"Don't do this, Bryony," she said. "You're going to get caught. You may have gotten away with Johnny's murder, but you won't get away with this."

"Oh, yes, I will," said Bryony with a strangely stilted smile. "I'm getting the hang of this, you know. It's true what they say about murder. Once you've made your first kill, the next ones are so much easier."

"The next ones? You're not thinking about killing again, are you?"

"Of course. Do you really think I want to see my daughter marry a drug dealer? When I kill Mr. Rubb I intend to inflict as much pain as possible. Serves him right for dealing my husband drugs and seducing my only daughter.

Now close your eyes and say a prayer. This is the end of the line."

"Just what I was going to tell you," a voice suddenly sounded behind Bryony. "Drop it!" the voice added sharply, "Or I drop you!"

When Odelia opened her eyes, she saw that Chase was standing in the doorway, pointing a very large gun at Bryony, who'd whirled around. The moment she caught sight of the large cop, she uttered a cry of dismay, and instantly dropped the gun. Not such a cold-blooded killer after all.

"Odelia, are you all right?" he asked, giving Bryony's gun a kick.

"I'm fine," she said, getting up. "I was just taking a nap while Bryony here told me the story of her life."

"You're under arrest, Mrs. Pistol," Chase grunted, and quickly and efficiently outfitted Bryony with a pair of handcuffs.

"How did you get here?" asked Odelia, surprised and extremely relieved.

"After you left I thought about what you said. All that stuff about not giving up. So I decided you were probably right. I figured I might as well try to get Veronica to sign a written confession fingering the Commissioner. When I arrived I saw your car parked out front, and the gate wide open. And when I looked through the window, I saw Mrs. Pistol here brandishing her gun." He gave Bryony a grim look. "Before you kill people you might want to close the curtains."

"Beginner's mistake," muttered the woman, looking extremely annoyed.

"You got here just in time," Odelia said. "Another minute and she would have put a hole in me."

"I figured as much when I saw you lying on that piece of plastic."

Just then, Odelia's phone beeped and she took it out.

"What is it?" asked Chase.

She smiled. "Um… is it all right if we take a little detour before we drop Mrs. Pistol off at the police station?"

He looked puzzled. "Why? You want to go for pizza?"

"Just a small errand I have to run. But a very urgent one. Let's go."

He shook his head. "You're speaking in riddles, Poole, as usual."

"Probably the reporter in me. Now let's get moving before it's too late."

She drove first, with Chase following right behind her, Bryony safely tucked in the backseat. She followed the flickering dot on the screen, and soon saw they were heading to the Writer's Lodge. Huh? What was Max doing out there? She drove at a healthy clip, and soon the two cars were roaring up the hill, the wheels of the two pickup trucks tackling the rutted dirt road and spraying up a cloud of dust. The road meandered and narrowed until they reached the small parking space right below the ridge where the Writer's Lodge was located.

She saw that two other cars were already parked there: a silver Mercedes and a burgundy BMW. She cut the engine and got out of the car, Chase joining her. He was staring at the Mercedes. "NYPD plates," he grunted.

She smiled, starting to see what was going on here. "Surprise, surprise."

He narrowed his eyes at her. "What are you up to, Poole?"

"Let's wait and see," she said, and set foot for the steps that led up from the small parking space to the lodge. She wondered where Max and the others could be. Probably in the shrubbery behind the lodge. So she made her way over there, and when she arrived, saw she hadn't been mistaken: Max, Dooley, Harriet and Brutus met her behind the lodge, right next to the verandah where Hetta Fried, the Lodge's owner, had installed the Jacuzzi.

She crouched down next to the cats, scratching Max behind the ears. She wasn't going to talk feline now, with Chase looking on, but pricked up her ears when Max said, "Better take out your camera," and pointed at the lodge.

She looked over, and saw a man and a woman enjoying the Jacuzzi.

"Well, I'll be damned," Chase whispered. "That's Commissioner Necker. And Malka Putin. Talk about a déjà-vu."

And as they approached the verandah, she saw the couple were doing things no married man and woman should do, at least not to the ones they weren't married to. With a grin, she took out her phone and started snapping pictures of the adulterous couple, adding a short video for good measure.

"I have a feeling Commissioner Necker will be a lot more amenable to finding a solution for your problems than before," she whispered to Chase.

"Let's go and say hi," Chase said.

"Wait, don't!" she hissed, but he was already walking up the two wooden steps to the verandah and pushing open the screen door.

When the startled couple looked up in dismay, he said, "Hi there, Commissioner. Remember me?"

"What the hell, Kingsley!" cried the Commissioner, descending beneath the bubbles. "You'll pay for this!"

"Not this time," Chase said, and when Odelia popped out from behind Chase's broad back, she flashed the Commissioner and Mrs. Putin her best smile and showed them her smartphone.

"Chase and I were out hiking in the woods, when we just happened upon you two love birds. So I decided to snap some shots. And a little video."

"Who are you?!" demanded the Commissioner, his face reddening.

"My name is Odelia Poole. I'm a reporter for the Hampton Cove Gazette and, as it happens, I've got an entire front page to fill in tomorrow's edition."

"Oh, Christ," muttered the Commissioner.

"This is all your fault!" cried Mrs. Putin. "I told you we should have booked a hotel!"

"Nobody ever comes out here!" yelled the Commissioner.

"Apart from a cop and a reporter, you mean?"

"Look," said Chase now, "I have absolutely no interest in exposing your little affair to the world, which is what I told you the last time, remember?"

"I remember," said the Commissioner, glaring at Odelia's smartphone.

"But you wouldn't listen, would you? And then you kicked me out."

"Yeah, yeah, yeah," grumbled the portly cop. "What do you want?"

"I want you to clear my name," said Chase.

The Commissioner looked surprised. "That's all?"

"Of course it's not all," said Mrs. Putin, a round-faced woman with platinum hair. "They want money, can't you see? How much do you want?"

"Shut up, Malka. Let me handle this."

"Look, I've got a hundred bucks right here," said the woman, reaching for her purse, which was right next to the bubble bath.

"Just let me handle this, all right?" cried the Commissioner.

"I don't want any money," said Chase now, shaking his head disgustedly. "I just want to clear my name. I want you to go on record and—"

"Done," said the Commissioner. "Whatever you want, son.

Anything. Just don't print those pictures, will you? They would ruin my career."

"What about me?" asked Mrs. Putin. "What about my reputation, huh? It's always me, me, me. You and my husband are just the same."

"Just shut up for a minute, will you? I'm handling this."

"That's what you said the first time," she said, crossing her arms.

"Look, Chase, I'll clear your record, all right? I'll talk to this girl—what's her name, ahm…"

"Veronica George," Odelia supplied helpfully.

"That's all right," said Chase. "Odelia already made arrangements with Miss George, and Mr. Rubb."

"She did?" asked the Commissioner, surprised. "You're some reporter, Miss…"

"Poole. Odelia Poole."

He frowned. "The name sounds familiar. Why does the name sound familiar?"

"Perhaps because Donovan Rubb called you to complain about being arrested?" she asked. "At which point you pressured the mayor into getting Chase fired. Again."

"Yeah. Yeah, yeah, yeah," he said, looking appropriately contrite. "Look, all that stuff wasn't my idea in the first place, all right?"

"Oh, now you're blaming me?" asked Mrs. Putin. "Nice. Real nice."

"I'm blaming your husband, that's who I'm blaming. Boyce set this up."

"Look, I don't care who set up whom," said Chase now. "All I care about is that my name is cleared and that you put an end to those rumors."

"Sure, sure, Chase. Whatever you want, son. I'll get you your job back, I'll even throw in a nice promotion and a nice big fat pay raise, all right?"

Odelia looked at Chase. Being reinstated as an NYPD detective was all Chase had ever wanted. But it would also mean leaving Hampton Cove, and she wasn't sure how she felt about that. She was surprised when she heard him say, "That's all right, Commissioner. I'm fine out here in Hampton Cove."

"Are you sure?" asked the Commissioner.

"He said he was sure, didn't he? Now delete those pictures already."

"Can you just shut up for one minute? I'm handling this."

"You can't even handle your way out of a paper bag," she grumbled.

"Yes, I'm sure," said Chase now. "I like it out here. A lot less hassle."

"Suit yourself," said the Commissioner. "If you want Hampton Cove, Hampton Cove is what you get. I'll talk to the guy in charge here, um, what's his name…"

"Chief Alec," Odelia supplied.

"That's right. I'll tell him to take you back. Now about those pictures…"

"I think I'll hang on to those for now," Odelia said. "Just until I'm sure you're keeping your end of the bargain."

"Oh, I'll keep my word," said the Commissioner. "I'll get you sorted out."

"That sounds great, Vernon," said Chase, and Odelia was surprised Chase was on a first-name basis with the Commissioner. He'd never told her.

"Look, I'm sorry, all right? I should never have made that damn deal."

"Especially since you knew damn well I wasn't going to talk," said Chase.

"It wasn't just me," said the Commissioner. "When Boyce found out…"

"I understand," said Chase. "It's all about politics, right?"

"It is," said the Commissioner with a shake of the head. "Back when your father and I were still walking the beat, me as a rookie and he as the seasoned vet, things were different. Once you get to my level, it's all about politics, son." He eyed Chase ruefully. "I'm sorry. I'm going to set the record straight."

Chase nodded once, and then promptly turned around and walked away.

"I'm just gonna, um…" Odelia said, and then quickly followed Chase.

"You're not gonna let that guy off the hook so easy, are you?" cried Malka Putin. "He'll talk, I told you. All cops talk. Jabbermouths, the lot of them."

"Not Chase Kingsley," grunted the Commissioner. "And now will you just shut up for once and listen to me?"

Odelia smiled to herself as she rounded the lodge. Those two made a great couple. They should have their own show. She quickly caught up with Chase.

"How did this happen?" Chase asked when she fell into step beside him.

"How did what happen?"

"How did we get out here just when the Commissioner and Malka Putin were holed up in there?" He eyed her suspiciously. "Are you with the NSA? CIA? FBI? Did you put a tracking device on Vernon's car or something?"

She laughed as they reached the clearing and descended the few steps to the parking lot. "Yes, I used a tracker, but no, I'm not with any agency."

"How did you plant a tracker on Vernon's car?"

She wondered how much to tell him, then decided the less he knew the better. He'd never believe her, and would probably think she was nuts.

"I put a tracker on Max, as he has a habit to wander off and get lost. A tracker and a panic button, actually. So when he triggered the alarm I knew we better come out here and get him before he started to panic."

He stared at her. "So you had no idea Vernon would be here?"

"Nope," she said, trying her darndest to keep a straight face. "Complete coincidence. Pretty amazing, huh?"

He shook his head. "You're something else, Odelia Poole, has anyone ever told you that?"

"Yes, they have, but I don't mind hearing it again."

"Well, you are," he said, leaning against the truck while he studied her intently. "So you're saying your cat just so happened to be out here when Vernon and Malka Putin were going at it, and he just so happened to trigger the alarm, putting you in the perfect position to snap those shots?"

"Yep," she said blithely. "That's cats for you. They will amaze you."

"They sure will." He stared at her, and she noticed for the first time that his blue eyes were flecked with green. He was pretty amazing himself. Then he shook his head and smiled, flashing those dimples at her. "You should have been a cop, Odelia. Are you sure you don't want to join the force? I bet we'd make one hell of a team."

"What would Dan do without me? I'm the only reporter he's got."

"He'll find someone else."

"Why don't I stay a reporter and we can still be one hell of a team?"

He grinned. "Teaming up with the world's nosiest reporter, huh?"

"Why not? This is Hampton Cove, Detective. We do things—"

"—a little differently out here. Yeah, I got the memo."

He was leaning in now, and for a moment she thought he might kiss her. But then a sharp voice sounded from behind them. "How long do I have to sit here in this stinking truck?! I have rights! I demand to see my lawyer!"

Chase patted the truck and moved away. "Duty calls, Poole."

"If I'm not mistaken it's the black widow calling."

He cocked his index finger at her and lithely rounded the truck and slid behind the wheel. "This time you follow me, Poole. No more surprises."

"Yes, sir," she said, tipping an imaginary cap.

She climbed into her own pickup and let the four cats in behind her. They jumped up onto the backseat and she slammed the door shut, then put the car in gear and drove off in Chase's wake.

"You guys did great," she told the fearsome feline foursome.

"Is Chase staying?" asked Harriet eagerly.

"He is."

"Oh, thank God," said Brutus.

"Thank Max," said Odelia. "He's the one who got us out here."

"Thank you, Max," said Harriet. ·

"Yeah, thanks, Maxie, baby," grunted Brutus, then held up his paw. "Hit me, bro."

"Oh, God," muttered Max, rolling his eyes, but then he did as instructed and gave Brutus a high five.

Odelia, watching the cats through the rearview mirror, noticed that Dooley was the only one who wasn't smiling. "What's wrong, Dooley? Cat got your tongue?"

"Ha ha. Very funny. Max scratched my nose. It hurts."

"All for a good cause, Dooley," said Max.

"Yes, you'll get over it, Dooley," said Harriet.

"It's called taking one for the team, Dooley, baby," said Brutus.

"I'm not a baby!"

"Oh, yes, you are, you big baby," Harriet cooed, and gave Dooley a peck on the whiskers. It perked him up considerably and he touched the spot reverently.

"We make a great team, you guys," said Brutus. "A great team with a great leader." He thumped his chest. "Yours truly. Bruce is back!"

"Oh, God," muttered both Dooley and Max.

Odelia smiled. The four cats had accomplished the seemingly impossible: expose the Commissioner's affair and exonerate Chase. And as she turned on the radio, a song of John Paul George came on.

"*I'm Your Bi-ba-boy*," the singer crooned. "*Your bi-ba-bad bad boy.*"

Soon, they were all singing along, four cats and one human giving John Paul George a run for his money. Pop music had never sounded so bi-ba-bad.

## Prologue

Clarice casually licked her paws. She'd snapped up a few morsels and was taking a breather on the windowsill. Overhead, a full moon shone, and inside the house all was quiet. Just the way she liked it. Word in town had it there were rodents to be found at the beach house, and word hadn't lied. She'd snapped up a few critters and decided this place was a keeper. Usually she liked to hang out in the hills west of Hampton Cove, but since she owed allegiance to no one, being a free spirit and all, she went where she pleased.

Clarice was a feral cat, her hide a mottled reddish brown riddled with bald spots. Once, she'd belonged to someone. Some tourists passing through who'd gotten her for their kid. When she'd gotten sick in the back of their Toyota Camry they'd decided she was more trouble than she was worth, and had tied her to a tree and left her. Good thing some kind soul had come along and freed her, or she would still be fettered to that damn tree, chewing bark.

The beach house was a property that had recently gone

through a major renovation. They'd taken a worn-out beach-front property, completely gutted it and turned it into a remarkable success story. Currently it was occupied by a sprawling family of exceedingly attractive females who'd come straight down here from Hollywood to film some scenes for a popular reality show. The three sisters lived in the main house while a small film crew had taken up lodgings in the guest house. The house was guarded twenty-four seven, but since no one ever stopped to frisk a cat, Clarice had easily slipped in and out.

Luckily for her the sisters didn't own a cat. Unfortunately what they did own was a nasty little yapper. A French Bulldog named Kane, who'd practically given her a heart attack when she'd entered the kitchen looking for some tasty little snack. The pooch wouldn't stop yapping. Sheesh. You'd think he had to pay for the food out of his own pocket. Good thing she knew how to handle a bully. She'd given him her best hiss and claw routine and he'd quickly run off with his tail between his legs, crying for his mommy.

She now sat licking her claws, savoring those final pieces of rat guts, when she noticed that something was going on inside the bedroom. She stared through the window and saw that someone had decided to play dress-up. They were donning a black gown that extended all the way to the feet and even covered the face, leaving only a tiny slit for the eyes.

The masked person was standing at the foot of the bed, staring down at the sleeping forms of one of the sisters and her husband. Way creepy.

She watched intently as the intruder brought out a rag and a small bottle and sloshed some liquid on the rag, then walked around the bed and pressed the rag against the face of the man, then reached over and repeated the procedure on the woman. This was no game. He or she was sedating them.

And then it got really freaky. Whoever was beneath that black robe suddenly reached inside the folds and brought out a shiny meat cleaver.

Clarice's eyes went wide with horror and shock when the robed intruder heaved the cleaver high and then let it drop down with a sickening thud on the woman's neck. Ouch! She cut her eyes to the French Bulldog lying at the foot of the bed. The stupid mongrel was stoically staring at the scene as if everything was hunky-dory. How weird was that? And as she watched, she felt a little sick to the stomach. She knew all humans were nuts and some were a little twisted, like the guy who'd tied her to that tree back in the day. But this was beyond sick. This was some evil *Game of Thrones* stuff right there. After a while, she had to look away, her stomach lurching. And since she was Hampton Cove's resident Feral Feline, that was saying something.

When Damien woke up it was as much from the rays of sun caressing his tan face as from the strong sense of nausea that assaulted him. It reminded him of that time he'd had plastic surgery, creating a cleft in his chin he'd hoped would add to his general look of cool dudiness. He'd woken up feeling just as nauseous from the anesthesia as he was feeling now. And then there was that smell. A pungent odor filling his nostrils and making him gag.

He groaned and rubbed his face. Did he have too much to drink last night? Nope. He and Shana had sat on the porch while her sisters cavorted in the pool. He hadn't felt like jumping in and neither had Shana. They'd had a huge fight, and neither had felt like having a romp in the pool or the Jacuzzi.

He cast a quick glance at his wife and saw she was fast

asleep, judging from the bump under the sheets. Oh, Christ, he just hoped she wouldn't start screaming again. He hated when she did that. There was no real argument possible when she screamed her head off. The sense of annoyance suddenly returned when he thought about the predicament she'd placed them both in.

With a sigh, he swung his feet to the hardwood floor, fisting his toes.

Wow. He had to hold onto his head when a sense of vertigo assaulted him. It was as if the entire room was spinning out of control. He had no idea what was going on, but judging from that horrible taste in his mouth and that terrible smell, things definitely were not A-okay.

He stalked off to the en-suite bathroom and stuck his head under the tap, allowing the water to run over his close-cropped hair and into the marble sink. The cold water did him a world of good, and he almost felt human again. He toweled off his head and checked his face in the mirror. His skin was blotchy, eyes bloodshot. Nothing some makeup couldn't fix. Good thing the camera crew wasn't filming. He so didn't want to go on TV looking like this. People would think he'd had too much nose candy last night. Which he hadn't. With a marriage on the rocks he had no appetite for the stuff. If he got divorced, all of this would go away. No more Mr. Big Shot Fancy Pants.

He walked back into the room and was surprised Shana wasn't up yet. All his stomping around and putting his head under the tap should have roused her by now. He took a deep breath and decided to get this over with. The mornings after a big fight were always the worst. He didn't know what to say and neither did she. Better to address the elephant in the room right away.

He sat down on the bed and gently shook her shoulder. "Shana, we need to talk," he said. When she didn't stir, he gave her a slight nudge. "Shana? Come on, honey. Things can't go on like this. I need some answers. Stat."

With a frown he noticed a spot of crimson on her pillow and he started. What the hell... He slowly slid down the sheet to take a closer look. And as he did, his eyes went wide and all the blood drained from his face. He would have screamed but no sound came. Later he didn't even remember staggering from the bed, falling to the floor and scrambling back, crab-style, to the door.

Like bile, a scream finally rose from his throat, coinciding with a scream that sounded from inside the house. He was up and racing down the corridor, and as he came hurtling into the dining room he saw Shayonne screaming her head off. When he turned to see what had set her off, he joined her in a long, protracted wail. Right there, in the middle of the table, was Shana's head, her eyes closed as if she were sleeping, her mouth open and biting down on a Jonagold, like a frickin' pig roast. A note was taped to her forehead, typed in Arabic script. And then he fainted and went down like a ton of bricks.

**Chapter One**

Dooley, Harriet and I were seated next to the bed, staring up at our human, who was still fast asleep, even snoring a little. When Odelia Poole had taken me in, I'd vowed a sacred oath never to let her be late for work. And even though keeping my promise was a lot harder than I'd anticipated, on account of the fact that Odelia slept like the dead, I wasn't giving up.

I'd snuggled up to her, digging my claws into her arm while purring in her hair. I'd mewled, meowed and mewed up a storm. I'd even scratched the closet door, pounding it in a steady rhythm, and all I had to show for my efforts was

Odelia muttering something unintelligible and turning over.

"She looks cute," Dooley said.

"Is she drooling?" Harriet asked.

"She always drools when she sleeps," I said.

"I think it's cute. She's almost like us," said Dooley.

"Not me," said Harriet. "I don't drool in my sleep."

"You snore, though," said Dooley. "It's so cute."

"Snoring isn't cute, and I don't snore."

"You do, too. Soft, little snuffles. Like a cute, little hamster."

"I'm not a hamster!"

"I didn't say you were a hamster. I said you sound like one. A cute one."

We went back to staring at Odelia. Her blond hair was a mess, her pixie face full of sleep marks, and her sheets were twisted and tangled as if she'd fought off Darth Vader in her sleep. And there was definitely drool. A lot of drool. As if she'd tried to scare off the Dark Lord by spitting at his helmet.

"All right," I said. "It's almost nine o'clock. She's going to be late."

The three of us were seated on the fuzzy pink bedside rug and could have sat there indefinitely, as the rug's softness felt great beneath my tush. But we had a responsibility. Being a cat isn't just about catching critters and looking cool doing it. It's about taking care of our humans while they're taking care of us. At least that's the way I see it. I may be an exception to the rule.

My name is Max, by the way, and I'm a blorange tabby. Yes, you read that right. I'm blorange. It's a color. It really is. A kind of strawberry blond.

"I think this calls for a serenade," Harriet said, licking her snowy white fur. She's a Persian, and pretty much the prettiest cat for miles around. She belongs to Odelia's mother, who lives next door, but she's in here all the time.

"A serenade?" asked Dooley. "What do you mean, a serenade?"

Dooley is a beige ragamuffin. You know, the kind that looks like a big, furry rabbit. Only he looks like a small, furry rabbit. A beige-and-white furry rabbit. Dooley is my best friend and neighbor. He comes with Odelia's grandma, who also lives next door. Yep. We're one big, happy family.

"I mean, a genuine serenade, like Romeo sang to Juliet?"

"Who's Romeo?" Dooley asked suspiciously. Dooley is secretly—or not-so-secretly—in love with Harriet, and jealous of every cat sniffing around.

Harriet rolled her eyes. "Romeo is a fictional character in a Shakespeare play. Don't you know anything, Dooley?"

Dooley raised his chin. "I know plenty. I know that Shakespeare is some dude who's in love, that's what I know. In love with Gwyneth Paltrow."

"That's not the real Shakespeare," Harriet huffed. "That's just a movie."

"Well, I don't see the point. There was no singing in the movie at all."

"I think Harriet is right," I said, deciding this was not the time for bickering. "We need to serenade Odelia. She loves our singing so much she'll wake up the moment she hears our sweet voices. Just like a radio clock."

"What's a radio clock?" asked Dooley.

"Oh, go away, Dooley," said Harriet. "Why don't we try the song we practiced last night? I'm sure she'll love it. She'll wake up gently and in a wonderful mood, completely refreshed. Like you said, just like a radio clock, but without those annoying radio jockeys jabbering about the weather."

"You mean *Sorry?*" I asked. "I don't think that's such a good idea."

"Why not? It was a big hit for Justin. I'm sure Odelia will love it."

"Who's Justin?"

"Oh, Dooley," Harriet sighed.

I stared at her. "Do you really think that song is appropriate?"

She laughed. "Appropriate? When is a love song *not* appropriate?"

"When is it?" asked Dooley, who had disliked the song as much as I had.

The thing is, Dooley and I had started cat choir a little while back, and had picked out a repertoire of cat-themed songs. You know, like *What's New Pussycat*. But when Harriet joined us she decided to glam up our repertoire, whatever that means. And then her boyfriend Brutus came along and took over conductor duties from Shanille, Father Reilly's tabby.

Things went downhill from there. Harriet started to dictate song choice, relying heavily on her mood. Last night she and Brutus had had a fight, and the big lug had us practicing Justin Bieber's *Sorry* all night. Oh, the horror.

We'd still managed, though, much to the chagrin of the neighbors, who hadn't liked our version as much as Harriet had. She'd been moved to tears when Brutus performed his solo and had responded by giving a rousing rendition of Celine Dion's *My Heart Will Go On*. It was all very disturbing.

"Oh, all right," I finally said. "Let's give it a try."

"Let's give what a try?" another voice now piped up behind us. I didn't even have to turn to know who the voice belonged to. Brutus happens to be my personal nemesis. The big black cat belongs to Chase Kingsley, who's the newest addition to the Hampton Cove police department, and has been making my life miserable ever since he arrived in town. He likes to think that just because his human is a cop he can lay down the law. And to add insult to injury, he's managed to snag Harriet's heart and dash all of Dooley's hopes.

"Oh, Brutus, sweetie," Harriet cooed. "We were about to try out that wonderful new song you taught us last night."

"That's a great idea, honey bunch," he said in that gruff voice of his.

He punched me on the shoulder, slapped Dooley on the back, and we both toppled over. "Let's do this, fellas," he growled, and cleared his throat.

Brutus is just about the worst choice when it comes to conducting a choir. The cat doesn't have a single musical bone in his big-boned body. But that doesn't stop him from belting his heart out every time he opens his mouth.

I shook my head. At least when Brutus decided to tackle Justin Bieber, Odelia would finally wake up. Judging from the dozens of angry neighbors last night, and the half dozen shoes thrown at our heads, it was hard to sleep through the racket. Then again, waking up Odelia was what we were here for. She'd told me yesterday the Hampton Cove Gazette is going through a rough patch. Circulation is down, so she needs to buckle down and find a killer story. And the first rule to finding a killer story is getting out of bed.

"One, two, three," Brutus grunted. He'd taken position in front of us, his back to Odelia, like a genuine conductor. He was even swinging his paw just so, claws extended in case we hit a wrong note. Brutus believes in tough love.

"*Is it too late now to say sorry?*" Brutus bellowed at the top of his lungs. He was eyeing Harriet intently, who was giggling more than she was singing.

"*Cause I'm missing more than just your body,*" she responded coyly.

"Oh, God," Dooley muttered.

"Hey! No bungling the lyrics!" Brutus yelled. "Be a Belieber!"

"I'm a Bebrutuser," Harriet tittered. "Is that all right, too?"

"It sure is, cutie pie," growled Brutus.

"Oh, God," I murmured.

"Hey!" Brutus repeated, and he slapped me on the head.

"Hey!" I yelled back. "No hitting the talent!"

"Who are you calling talent?" he said with a smirk.

"Oh, God," a tired voice came from behind Brutus.

He whirled around, ready to admonish her. But when he saw he wasn't talking to one of his choir flunkies, he snarled, "Look who's up!" instead.

"What was that racket?" she groaned.

"*Sorry*," said Harriet.

"That's okay. Just don't do it again."

"No, that's the name of the song."

"You could have fooled me," Odelia said, rubbing her eyes. "It sounded like a dozen cats being strangled, their heads chopped off with a lightsaber."

I know I should have felt offended, but I was so glad she was finally up I decided to forgive her. Not everyone appreciates great music the way us cats do, and the most important thing was that we'd finally achieved our purpose.

"Rise and shine, sleepyhead," I said. "Time to go to work."

"Ugh," was Odelia's response. "Just promise never to sing to me again."

"I promise," I said, crossing my claws. Until next time.

## Chapter Two

I was glad we'd accomplished our mission, even though the awakening hadn't been as gentle and pleasant as I'd hoped. Odelia obviously wasn't a fan of cat choir, or Justin Bieber, or either. We probably needed to practice more. Then again, with Brutus at the helm we might never get to be as good as the Wiener Sängerknaben, my inspiration to start cat choir in the first place. Especially if Brutus kept hogging the spotlight to impress Harriet. It didn't impress the other choir members. And it didn't impress me.

We trudged down the stairs and padded into the kitchen, waiting for Odelia to join us, fresh from the shower and ready to start preparing breakfast. We didn't have to wait long. She breezed in, wearing ultra-short Daisy Dukes, pockets showing on the bottom, a canary yellow T-shirt that announced she was 'Crazy Cat Lady' and pink Converse sneakers. She started up the coffeemaker and switched on the TV to watch the news.

"Ugh. The Kenspeckles are still in town," she said as she dumped Corn Flakes into a bowl and poured milk on top of it and a few spoonfuls of sugar. "I keep hoping they'll leave, but that obviously isn't happening."

"Who are the Kenspeckles?" asked Dooley.

We'd all hopped up on the kitchen counter barstools and were watching Odelia's breakfast preparations intently. As soon as she'd finished preparing her own breakfast, we knew she'd start on ours.

"Just some family whose lives have been turned into a reality show," she said. "The only reason I'm interested is because they decided to spend the summer in Hampton Cove and Dan keeps pushing me to do a piece on them. I'd rather poke my eye out with a fork than to come anywhere near them."

"Why Hampton Cove?" I asked.

She shrugged. "Cause it's the Hamptons. Cause it's the place where all the cool people hang out. Cause after shooting a gazillion shows in LA they like to shake things up. I don't know and I don't care. I'm not a fan."

That much was obvious. "You don't like the Kenspeckles?" asked Harriet.

"Nope. Too much talk. I like a show with a little action and a great story."

"Like *Game of Thrones*," said Brutus, nodding.

"Yuck. A show where people's heads get chopped off? No way."

"I know what you like," said Brutus. "You like to watch the game."

She stared at him. "Game? What game?"

"Football, of course! At Casa Chase we watch it all the time."

"At Casa Odelia we watch *The Voice*," I said.

Brutus made a face. "*The Voice*? Are you crazy?"

"It's all about singing, Brutus. I wouldn't expect you to understand."

"I like singing," he said with a quick glance at Harriet. "In fact, I love it. But *The Voice*? I thought you said you liked action and a great story, Odelia?"

"It doesn't get any better than Blake and Adam," she said, taking a seat and scooping up her flakes. "Add in some great songs and I'm hooked."

Brutus shook his head. It was obvious he didn't agree. "To each his own."

The sliding glass door in the living room opened and Odelia's mom walked in. "Good morning, family. And what a glorious morning it is."

A slim woman with long blond hair just like her daughter, Marge Poole was wearing hers in a messy bun this morning. Her white polka-dot shirt was belted with a thin leather sash and she was donning skinny black slacks. She gazed at us through horn-rimmed glasses and gave us a smile and a wave.

"Hey, Mom," said Odelia. "Aren't you the sight for sore eyes?"

"Oh, just my work clothes," said Mom with a deferential gesture.

Marge Poole was a librarian and ran the Hampton Cove library.

"I'd certainly borrow a book from you, Mrs. P," said Dooley.

"Dooley!" Harriet hissed.

"What? I would," said Dooley.

"She's a human and you're a feline. That's just wrong."

He frowned. "Why can't I borrow a book from her? I know my ABCs."

"Oh, you mean an actual book?"

"Of course. Why else would I go to the library?"

"I just thought..." She rolled her eyes. "Never mind."

"We were just talking about Chase," said Brutus.

"No, we weren't," said Odelia. "We were talking about the Kenspeckles."

"Chase is such a nice young man," Marge said. "And such a blessing for this town. Your uncle Alec keeps telling me he's so glad Chase decided to stay put instead of going back to New York to shoot with the big boys."

"Run with the big boys," Odelia corrected automatically.

"That's what I said. He could have had any job he wanted with the NYPD but he chose to stay in Hampton Cove. Isn't that just wonderful?"

"Super," Odelia murmured. "They should give him the keys to the city."

"I'm sure glad he stayed," said Harriet, practicing her best starry-eyed look on Brutus. "I don't know what I would do without my Brutus."

"Me neither, honey bunch," said Brutus.

Mom stood watching the syrupy scene with cocked head. "Aw, isn't that sweet? Young love."

"It's the best," muttered Odelia, not impressed.

"Shouldn't you be home with Chase right now?" I asked Brutus.

"Yeah, he'll wonder where you are," said Dooley.

"I'm sure he doesn't mind me spending the night with my girlfriend."

"I'm sure he doesn't," said Marge. "Chase strikes me as a man who appreciates love and affection. For a police officer he's very much in touch with his feelings." She gave Odelia a meaningful look.

Odelia threw up her hands. "Don't hold anything back, Mom."

"Well, I won't. Detective Kingsley is a wonderful young man, extremely handsome and very sweet and you could do a lot worse than him. And he's single, which I'm sure he won't be for long so you better move fast."

"I told you already. I'm not interested in Chase Kingsley."

"Someone else might snap him up. Alec tells me Blanche Captor comes into the office every day to file littering charges. She's in there at the crack of dawn, demanding Chase take her statement. And she just had that boob job."

"I'm sure it takes more than a pair of boobs to turn Chase's head, Mom."

"I'm not so sure. Chase might be a great guy but he's still a guy. And you know what that means." She directed a pointed glance at Odelia's more modest chest. "The women in our family have to rely on other assets, honey."

"Oh, for crying out loud, Mom," Odelia groaned.

To be honest, I've never understood this obsession with boobs. I mean, I'm a guy and I don't care one hoot about them. Then again, I'm not human, so maybe that's why. Truth of the matter is that Odelia has dated a few lemons in the past, so she's understandably cautious and I don't blame her.

"I think Chase is dreamy," said Harriet, contradicting her

earlier statement that interspecies relationships are just plain wrong.

"And I think he's a great cop, but that doesn't mean he's relationship material," I said, deciding to put my two cents in. It seemed Odelia's dating life was a free-for-all now, so why not share my opinion with the group?

Mom laughed. "Oh, Max. Since when did you become an expert?"

I shrugged. "Just looking out for my human. Someone has to."

I like Marge, I really do, but I don't like how she tries to foist this cop on Odelia. To be honest, my motives weren't totally selfless. If Odelia hooked up with Chase, it wouldn't be long before he moved in and so would Brutus. If there was a way to prevent this doomsday scenario, I was all for it.

Marge patted me on the head. "You're doing a great job, Max."

"Thanks," I said dubiously. Compliments are a double-edged sword. You have to be careful or they blow up in your face. If it's swords that blow up in your face. It might be plans. I don't know. Hey, I'm a cat, not a dictionary.

"I think Odelia and Chase should hook up," said Harriet. "Just like Brutus and I have found each other. That way we'll all be family forever."

"I think you should listen to you cats, honey," said Mom. "They're a sacred and ancient species known far and wide for their infinite wisdom."

"I think Chase should return to wherever he came from," said Dooley, giving Brutus a particularly dirty look.

Odelia held up her hand. "All right, Mom. I'll listen to my wise cats."

"Dooley is confused, that's all. He is your grandmother's cat, after all. Some of her traits are bound to rub off on him and dilute his innate wisdom."

"I thought Gran wanted me to get together with Chase?"

"Gran wants to get together with Chase herself," said Marge with a tight-lipped smile. "Which is hardly appropriate for her age."

Odelia put her bowl in the sink. "You know what I think? This family is starting to resemble the Kenspeckles. If we're not careful we'll have our own reality show soon."

"Ooh, I'd like that," said Harriet. "I would love to be on TV."

"Oh dear God, no," said Marge. "Just imagine all those cameras filming everything we do. We wouldn't have a life anymore—no privacy at all!"

"It's all scripted," Odelia said. "Nothing about that show is real, Mom."

"Are you sure?"

"Of course I'm sure. Nobody behaves like that. It's completely fake."

"I think it's all real," said Harriet. "Especially the relationships. Nobody can fake all that love and affection. You can see it in their eyes."

Dooley and I rolled our own eyes. Odelia was right. Maybe *Keeping Up with the Pooles* would be the next big thing. Though *Keeping Up with Harriet and Brutus* would be an even bigger hit. Nobody could fake that much ignorance.

**Neighborhood Witch Committee**

Witchy Start

Witchy Worries

Witchy Wishes

**Saffron Diffley**

Crime and Retribution

Vice and Verdict

Felonies and Penalties (Saffron Diffley Short 1)

**The B-Team**

Once Upon a Spy

**Tate-à-Tate**

Enemy of the Tates

**Ghosts vs. Spies**

The Ghost Who Came in from the Cold

**Witchy Fingers**

Witchy Trouble

Witchy Hexations

Witchy Possessions

Witchy Riches

Box Set 1 (Books 1-4)

**The Mysteries of Bell & Whitehouse**

One Spoonful of Trouble

Two Scoops of Murder

Three Shots of Disaster

Box Set 1 (Books 1-3)

A Twist of Wraith

A Touch of Ghost

A Clash of Spooks

Box Set 2 (Books 4-6)

The Stuffing of Nightmares

A Breath of Dead Air

An Act of Hodd

Box Set 3 (Books 7-9)

A Game of Dons

**Standalone Novels**

When in Bruges

The Whiskered Spy

**ThrillFix**

Homejacking

The Eighth Billionaire

The Wrong Woman

# ABOUT NIC

Nic Saint is the pen name for writing couple Nick and Nicole Saint. They've penned 70+ novels in the romance, cat sleuth, middle grade, suspense, comedy and cozy mystery genres. Nicole has a background in accounting and Nick in political science and before being struck by the writing bug the Saints worked odd jobs around the world (including massage therapist in Mexico, gardener in Italy, restaurant manager in India, and Berlitz teacher in Belgium).

When they're not writing they enjoy Christmas-themed Hallmark movies (whether it's Christmas or not), all manner of pastry, comic books, a daily dose of yoga (to limber up those limbs), and spoiling their big red tomcat Tommy.

Sign up for the no-spam newsletter and be the first to know when a new book comes out: nicsaint.com/newsletter.

www.nicsaint.com

facebook.com/nicsaintauthor

twitter.com/nicsaintauthor

bookbub.com/authors/nic-saint

amazon.com/author/nicsaint

Made in United States
Orlando, FL
24 May 2023

33444592R00136